Elaine Singleton's body lay sprawled on the grass like an old doll discarded by a child, her arms and legs tossed about carelessly. Skeletal thin, the skin mottled with blue veins and brown spots, the white hair stuck up like old straw, her nightgown soiled and spotted with blackened cigarette holes, she *looked* like a used-up old doll.

The man who was looking at the body of Elaine Singleton was also old. He had come out of the building just a moment before. He was a short wiry man. On his head was a dark peaked cap that had NY written on it in off-white. Though seventy-three, he had that toughness that survived youth. In the elderly it was called feistiness. He looked at Elaine's body and shook his head sadly. It was not a pretty sight.

The man looked at the scene for a long moment. He couldn't turn and walk away . . .

MORE MYSTERIES FROM THE
BERKLEY PUBLISHING GROUP...

FORREST EVERS MYSTERIES: A former race-car driver solves the high-speed crimes of world-class racing . . . "A Dick Francis on wheels!"
—Jackie Stewart

by Bob Judd
BURN   SPIN
CURVE

THE REVEREND LUCAS HOLT MYSTERIES: They call him "The Rev," a name he earned as pastor of a Texas prison. Now he solves crimes with a group of reformed ex-cons . . .

by Charles Meyer
THE SAINTS OF GOD MURDERS   BLESSED ARE THE MERCILESS

FRED VICKERY MYSTERIES: Senior sleuth Fred Vickery has been around long enough to know where the bodies are buried in the small town of Cutler, Colorado . . .

by Sherry Lewis
NO PLACE FOR SECRETS   NO PLACE LIKE HOME
NO PLACE FOR SIN   NO PLACE FOR TEARS

INSPECTOR BANKS MYSTERIES: Award-winning British detective fiction at its finest . . . "Robinson's novels are habit-forming!"
—*West Coast Review of Books*

by Peter Robinson
THE HANGING VALLEY   FINAL ACCOUNT
WEDNESDAY'S CHILD   INNOCENT GRAVES
GALLOWS VIEW
PAST REASON HATED

JACK McMORROW MYSTERIES: The highly acclaimed series set in a Maine mill town and starring a newspaperman with a knack for crime solving . . . "Gerry Boyle is the genuine article."   —Robert B. Parker

by Gerry Boyle
DEADLINE   BLOODLINE
LIFELINE

SCOTLAND YARD MYSTERIES: Featuring Detective Superintendent Duncan Kincaid and his partner, Sergeant Gemma James . . . "Charming!"
—*New York Times Book Review*

by Deborah Crombie
A SHARE IN DEATH   ALL SHALL BE WELL
LEAVE THE GRAVE GREEN   MOURN NOT YOUR DEAD

OLD GANG OF MINE

RICHARD F. WEST

BERKLEY PRIME CRIME, NEW YORK

OLD GANG OF MINE

A Berkley Prime Crime Book / published by arrangement with the author

PRINTING HISTORY
Berkley Prime Crime edition / September 1997

The Putnam Berkley World Wide Web site address is http://www.berkley.com

ISBN: 0-425-15964-7

Berkley Prime Crime Books are published by The Berkley Publishing Group, a member of Penguin Putnam Inc., 200 Madison Avenue, New York, NY 10016.
The name BERKLEY PRIME CRIME and the BERKLEY PRIME CRIME design are trademarks belonging to Berkley Publishing Corporation.

PRINTED IN THE UNITED STATES OF AMERICA

10 9 8 7 6 5 4 3 2 1

For Mom and Pop with love.
Mere words are inadequate to express
my gratitude for all the sacrifices they made for me.

Special thanks to Henny Youngman
for his cooperation on this work,
and for all the laughs over the years.

OLD GANG
OF MINE

CHAPTER

1

Elaine Singleton's body lay sprawled on the grass, her arms and legs tossed about carelessly like an old doll discarded by a child. Skeletal thin, skin mottled with blue veins and brown spots, white hair stuck up like old straw, her nightgown soiled and spotted with blackened cigarette holes, she *looked* like a used-up old doll.

The man looking at the body of Elaine Singleton was also old. Benny Ashe had come out of the building just a moment before. He was a short, wiry man. Though seventy-three, he had a toughness that had survived youth. In the elderly, it was called feistiness. He was wearing well-worn sneakers, faded cotton pants, and a faded short-sleeved shirt. On his head was a dark, peaked cap that had NY written on it in off-white. He looked at Elaine's body and shook his head sadly. It was not a pretty sight. It was made less pretty by the bright sun lighting up the world, causing every detail of Elaine Singleton's body to stand out sharply against the bright grass.

The man looked at the scene for a long moment as he tried to figure out just what to do. He couldn't turn and walk away. Yet, that was what he wanted to do. Mind his own business. But he couldn't bring himself to do it. It wasn't right. Especially because it was a woman. He'd been raised on the tough streets of Greenpoint in Brooklyn where he'd thought nothing of punching some guy who'd made him angry. He didn't have more than an eighth grade education, but the one thing he learned—and learned well—was to respect women. No matter how old, no matter how disreputable. He would hit a man without much provocation. He would never raise a hand to a woman. Women were to be protected and treated with dignity. So he couldn't turn his back on this one, no matter how much he wanted to. It was not in his nature. Well, he sighed in resignation, it was up to him to do something.

He went back through the door and headed down the long corridor on the first floor toward the lobby at the front of the building. It was a lobby fit for any upscale hotel. Done in soft pastels of muted pinks and reds, it vaulted three floors to a glass roof. The floor area was carpeted in rust-red and filled with sofas, brass tables, and plants. There was a glass elevator that went from the lobby up the three floors. This, however, was not a hotel, though in many ways it functioned like a hotel. This was Coral Sands, an assisted living retirement residence.

He went to the front desk, folded his arms and leaned on the brown counter top in front of where the desk clerk sat. She looked up at him. She was a tough-looking woman in her fifties, with dyed brown hair, a thick body, and a cold look.

"What do you need, Benny?" she said. Her voice was gentle and soft, the direct opposite of her hard appearance.

Benny Ashe looked at her, ready to tell her about Elaine Singleton, then he thought better of it. It was not right that they should see her that way. He knew that as soon as he told her, Grace would alert the staff and just about everyone would be outside staring at Elaine Singleton's body. It would be disgraceful. In the end, dignity was all people had left. The least he could do was protect that dignity.

"Never mind, Grace," he said. He left the desk and went in search of help. He moved about the game rooms, the coffee area, and the swimming pool before he was able to round up three other men. The three were younger than he, but they, too, were old. Together they walked around the building to the back where Elaine's body lay. At the sight of the body, each of the men shook his head sadly, just as Benny Ashe had.

"Not a pretty sight," one of them said.

The three men bent down, grunting as they did, and grabbed her. They held her legs together, tucking the nightgown around the legs to preserve her decency, then two of the men picked her up by the legs. The third man was larger and stronger looking than the other two, he had her by the shoulders. Benny Ashe held the door open for them.

"Boy, she really smells," the second man said, making a face. "They won't have to embalm her."

"For a skinny old lady she sure is heavy," the third man said, huffing with the weight.

"It's Newton's first law," the second man said. "Things get heavier as you get older."

"Wayne Newton said that?" the first man asked.

They struggled through the doorway and started up the stairs. The stairs were narrow and steep. That made it more difficult for the man holding Elaine's shoulders and climbing backward. Partway up he grunted for them to stop. Each was panting hard. They settled on the stairs. They were not used to this physical activity.

"This is tough work," one of them said.

"Be glad she doesn't weigh three hundred pounds."

"Three hundred pounds and I'd've left her where she was lying."

"Yeah. Plant a flower bed around her."

"I think I'm having a heart attack," said the first of the two men holding her legs. He was gasping for breath.

"Well, wait until we get to the top of the stairs. You keel over now and we'll all go falling down the stairs."

"You think I can pick the time when I have a heart attack?"

"Okay, let's do it," the man holding her shoulders said. "While Jimmy's heart is still working." He tightened his jaw, and braced himself to pick Elaine's body up again.

It was at that moment she opened her eyes with a snap.

"What the hell you guys doing to me!" The sour alcohol fumes that came out with the words had the men wincing and turning their faces away. "Put me down you bastards! What is this, a gang rape?" She struggled weakly to free herself. There was not enough strength to make it a real effort. "I'm going to report this to the police! Get your slimy hands off me! Dirty, foul men trying to take advantage of me!" Her voice was a weak, hoarse rasp filled with anger. Once started, she didn't stop hollering at them. "Let go of me! Help!" she screamed, but the sound was no louder than before. "Help! Rape! I'm being molested!"

The men exchanged looks that communicated a lot. The three of them shrugged, braced themselves, picked her up, and carried her back down the stairs. Benny Ashe was still at the door. He held it open for them.

"What are you doing? Put me down, you hear? I knew you guys were slime. Taking advantage of a defenseless woman! Put me down."

They carried her through the door to the outside.

"Why are you taking me outside! Stop this! I'm in my nightgown! Everybody will see me! Help me, somebody!

You guys are disgusting! Stop this, damn you!''

They carried her across the lawn to where they had found her, put her down on the grass, then turned and calmly walked away.

CHAPTER
2

"Spoons. Now it is spoons." The man spoke with just a hint of a Spanish accent, smooth tones where harsh sounds should have been. "That makes so far twelve." He was young, early twenties, short and dark, with black hair and gentle features. The apron didn't seem out of place on him, though it wrapped all the way around his lean body. He was standing in the doorway to the office. "Pretty soon we got to order some more, or we have none left for everybody."

"Who would be taking spoons?" Jessie Cummings was an attractive woman, though weight was being added in places she didn't like. Bulging fat was the image she had in her mind of women over forty. And she had just turned forty three weeks back. Over the hill. Though better over it than under it. A bottle of magic potion from the pharmacy kept her hair shiny black and youthful, but seeing the gray roots appearing made her aware that hiding her aging was a battle she would eventually lose. Today she wore a tan dress, with a severe military cut and a flap pocket over each breast, that she hoped was accentuating her shoulders and chest and hiding the bulges that were being added to the rest of her body. She was seated behind the desk in the little office she called home.

"The same person who took the knives," he said. He was annoyed, and that made his tone even softer and more deliberate. "And the salad forks. Now it is spoons. Someone is getting together a set of the silverware."

She frowned. It was a hesitant frown, as if she wasn't sure whether to frown or not. Her face looked pretty even when she frowned, and the frown accentuated her blue eyes. It was the kind of face, with clean firm lines, that said this woman was in charge. And her voice held the same authority. "But why? These people here have enough money to buy their own complete set of silverware. This is not a nursing home under Medicare. Everyone here had to put good solid money up front to live here, and they pay monthly to stay. And we did a thorough analysis of their assets before we invited them. We make sure they have the money so this won't be a hardship for them."

"At the rate they are taking the silverware it will not be a hardship for them." Manuel shook his head. "It will be a hardship for us. I told you, you get plastic things and nobody will steal them."

It was Jessie Cummings's turn to shake her head. "We can't have plastic utensils. The whole atmosphere here is of elegance. People need elegance in their life. It makes them feel good about themselves. The dining room is like an expensive restaurant, complete with tablecloths, cloth napkins, fine glassware and good china. And silver flatware."

"Except they will have to share the spoons," Manuel said. His expression was always calm, with a hint of a smile that said he was above all this.

"All right," she said, and sighed. "I give up. I'll order more spoons."

"Soon," he said.

"Soon," she agreed. "Today."

"*Gracias!*" he said. "I will start counting the plates. Maybe the thief is setting up a home for somebody." He grinned, shrugged, and left her office.

She smiled, but there was trouble behind the smile. She wasn't sure it wasn't Manuel taking the silverware. The only people who had to gain by stealing were the help. They were working for a living, and they were not high on the salary ladder. Worst of all they had to cater to a building filled with old people. It took a special kind of person to deal with the elderly. She didn't screen the kitchen help for those qualities when she hired them. Finding a competent cook, even a competent dishwasher like Manuel was hard enough without putting further restrictions on their qualifications.

The thievery was noticed only a week ago, and she didn't know what to do about it. The staff, except for two of the busboys, one waiter, and the cook had been with Coral Sands for over a year. Many for quite a few years. The cook, Raymond Bullon, had been with them only a couple of months, after Johnny Custer fell off the wagon and disappeared wherever alcoholics disappeared to. Johnny had access to the cutlery as well as the others. The waiter, Chris Lassiter, was new and temporary. He was replacing Carlos Ortega, who had smashed up his leg in a motorcycle accident, until Carlos was back on his feet. Chris, a friend of Carlos's, was a nice guy and seemed to enjoy the work. The busboys were indistinguishable: two guys, Mike and George, who looked like they were coming back from the place alcoholics disappear to. Quiet men, who did their jobs without complaint.

In Jessie's ten years at Coral Sands there had been a few cases of pilfering. In all those cases the thieves had been the maids who cleaned the rooms. Jessie had hired a private investigator and found it easy enough to locate the guilty parties, get the property back, and dismiss them. But there hadn't been anything for over two years. This pilfering of spoons was weird, and she didn't know how to handle it. It seemed silly to contact the police over missing spoons, and it would be cheaper to let the thief steal than hire a private investigator. Nothing was ever simple, she sighed wearily.

Jessie flipped through the Rolodex on her desk to the card with the name of the restaurant supplier she used. Then she checked the little clock on her desk—10:32 A.M. They should be up and operating. She picked up the phone and punched in the number from the card.

It was a clear day, bright with sunshine. A Florida day—picture perfect. Solid puffs of clouds in a sky of pure blue. In the soft breezes, the palm trees across the lake moved their fronds lazily like slow dancers. The surface of the lake was gently roughened with ripples from the wind, giving the reflection of the sky in its surface a fractured jigsaw-puzzle look. The broad view was spectacular. Florida had so many spectacular views.

Peter Benington stood behind the sliding glass doors of his apartment, taking in the view with each deep breath. Long slow breaths, deep satisfying sighs. A good day. Life had good days, and bad. This was one of the good ones, and he hoped it was the first of many more to come. One of the laws attributed to Murphy stated that "If you feel good, don't worry. You'll get over it." Peter Benington knew that was true. But the key was to take as much out of the times when you're feeling good to help you cope with bad times. This was one time he was going to milk for all it was worth.

The deep breaths and the long sighs covered a nervous excitement. Life was starting anew. The past was gone, never to be resurrected, he hoped.

He'd gotten in late the previous night, and since then had spent much of the time straightening the furniture and unpacking his things. The apartment didn't look like he had just moved in. Except, that is, for the flattened cartons stacked next to the door to the hall, and the two trash bags stuffed with packing paper that huddled against the cartons. He had wanted to get settled in quickly. It had taken a good part of the night, but he had finished. It was over, and it looked liked he had lived here for a long time. The space was new to him, but the furniture had made it his space. His furniture contained part of his spirit, held the essences of loving ghosts, and it made him feel he belonged.

It was close to ten. Later than he had wanted to be ready. He would have preferred to make his appearance at breakfast. But it couldn't be helped. He'd unpacked and put things away until well after three in the morning. And though he'd set the alarm for six-thirty, he slept right through until nine. Missed his medication as well as breakfast. Even as he was unpacking last night, he kept telling himself to quit and go to bed. But he knew he wouldn't be able to sleep. He was too excited. So, he had persevered. He shrugged, it will have to be lunch, instead of breakfast.

He'd had a cup of instant coffee at nine or so, first thing after he got up. He took his medication with the coffee. A little beta blocker "to calm his fluttering heart," he told the women. Then he cleaned out the cup, went into the bathroom, washed his face and shaved. He dressed in a pale yellow short-sleeved shirt and tan slacks with a matching tan belt, and tan, suede, crepe-soled shoes. He checked himself one more time in the mirror behind the door in the bedroom closet. The cat's meow. A little old. A little wrinkled. A little thick around the waist. Hair a bit thin and it was white, but it was enough to cover most of his head. And the thin, neatly trimmed mustache—also white—that drove the girls wild. He smiled. "You devil," he said aloud to his reflection.

He did one last check of his pockets to make sure he had everything. He opened the door to the hall, and moved the flattened cartons and the two trash bags outside in the hall, stacking it all next to the door. Then he took one deep fortifying breath, and left the apartment.

"Peter." The voice was soft and nearby.

He turned and faced the woman who was coming near him. Marjorie. A darling woman. He had been looking forward to seeing her again.

"Marjorie." He smiled. "How wonderful that you came to get me."

She stopped next to him, and he could see she was looking a little odd.

"I wish that was the case, Peter." There was a sheen of perspiration on her face. "The welcoming committee is waiting for you downstairs. But, I had to leave. Not feeling well. I'm heading for my apartment." Involuntarily her hand went to her stomach. "Something I ate, no doubt." She smiled reluctantly. "Been doing a little too much eating lately." Then her smile warmed and her eyes probed his. "I did so want to welcome you with the others."

He turned on his warmest smile. "I think you already adequately welcomed me last month when I came down to sign all the papers for this establishment."

Her face reddened, and her gaze slipped away for a moment.

She grinned shyly. "It was a wonderful evening wasn't it."

He reached out and placed a hand on her arm. "One I

will never forget. And I hope we can add many such evenings to our memories."

"You wonderful flatterer. Are all you English so flattering?" She made an effort to smile, then clutched her stomach, and winced. "Just the worst time to get sick. I must get to my room and lie down for awhile. Maybe it will all pass."

He stepped closer and took her arm. "Let me help you to your room." As he guided Marjorie slowly down the hall, he saw a fragile unkempt woman in a soiled nightgown and bare feet weaving down the hall toward them. The woman avoided their eyes and entered a room further down the hall. Peter looked to Marjorie for an explanation. Marjorie sighed wearily. "Elaine Singleton. She has an alcohol problem. Doesn't harm anyone. She keeps to herself, and we don't bother her. We are all too old to be reformers."

Peter leaned toward Marjorie. "I see you are wearing your beautiful diamond necklace today. Just for me?"

She smiled weakly. "Well, I don't go around in my jewels for breakfast. And you did so admire the necklace when I wore it at dinner last month."

"Ah, but it was you who made the necklace look its best, Marjorie."

"You're flattering me again. And I want you to promise me you'll never stop." She tried to smile, but the pain in her stomach stopped it from forming. She sucked in a hard breath.

They stopped outside of room 312. Peter opened the door, and helped Marjorie inside her apartment.

"It's okay, Peter. You can go downstairs. The others are waiting."

"Are you sure there is nothing I can do for you? Tuck you in, perhaps?"

She did manage a playful smile through the pain. "You wicked man. There will be plenty of time for you to do that when I get over this. Now go downstairs. The others are anxious to meet you."

"I assume you told them all about me, already?"

"Yes. And they want to see if I'm a liar." The pain stabbed suddenly, and she grabbed her stomach tightly with her hand. "Now, please go. I'll be all right."

He left her and walked down the hall—carpeted in a rich, dark red—to the elevator. There was a balcony in front of the elevator that circled around the huge open area two stories below. The area down below looked like the lobby of an expensive hotel, complete with luxurious plants, sofas, tables and stuffed chairs. The elevator hung out over that lobby. It was exciting to think that this was where he now lived. He could sit in that lobby any day, any time. Read the newspaper or just hang around, not having to worry about who might be coming up behind him.

He stepped into the all-glass elevator and pressed the button for the first floor. His heart began to kick up with the excitement. The doors closed smoothly, and the elevator slowly descended to the lobby. There the doors opened quietly, and he stepped off. The dining room was a few yards down the hall directly behind him. Over his shoulder he could see the staff moving about setting things up for lunch, which from the introductory literature he had received, was served from eleven-thirty to one-thirty.

"Hey, it's about time you came down." Benny Ashe had come up behind Peter. "Been looking for you all morning. Grace told us you moved in last might."

Peter turned to face Benny, and the first thing he saw was the dark baseball cap with NY over the bill. Peter tried to put a name to the face. Peter knew he had met the man when he had been given the tour of the place by Dolores Stevens, the saleswoman. But that must have been two months back.

"Benny Ashe," Benny said, and stuck out his hand. "We met when you first walked through the place."

"Yes, I remember," Peter said with a smile. "Peter Benington." He took Benny's hand, shook it and released it.

"Come on, I'll take you around and introduce you to some of the people. I'm kinda the official greeter around here. Been here almost fourteen years. Sorta know my way around. And all the people here know me. We got a sort of welcoming committee." With a nod, he indicated an area off to the side. "Want a cup of coffee?"

"Sounds like a great idea." Peter took two steps and was jolted from behind. "What the . . . ?"

A clown stood looking at him. "Sorry, buster, but clowns have the right of way." A thick voice like gravel came from the round white face with the big red smile and large red nose. The clown had a head of outrageously red curly hair, and was wearing a red and white checked outfit with big flappy shoes. "I mean, if you can't see me coming in this outfit, you got a problem with your eyes."

"Hey, Alice," Benny said. "Take it easy. Don't kill the new guy. This is Peter Benington. Just arrived today."

The clown extended a hand covered in a white glove, and Peter took it. "Pleased to meetcha," the clown said. "Alice Chomseky, clown extraordinaire. Wish I could stay and chat, but I'm on a mission."

"Another kid's party?" Benny said.

"Yeah. A bunch of brats screaming in my ear for an hour. Gotta go. Good meeting you," she said to Peter, then, before he could say anything, she hurried across the lobby toward the front door.

Peter, grinning in disbelief, watched her leave. She was

not exactly what he expected to see in a place like this. A short, thickset Cuban, neatly dressed, in dark glasses was coming through the front door. He dodged out of Alice's way, and looked after her with a perplexed expression. Peter knew exactly what the man was feeling.

"Don't mind her," Benny said. "She's a little rough, but she's real people. I think the tough part's an act, myself. She was a clown with the circus. Decided she didn't want to retire with circus people, so she came here. But she needs something to do, and she likes to make people laugh. So she does kid's parties and affairs at the hospital and such. Keeps her busy. Makes her feel needed." He looked at Peter and shrugged. "Something we all need." He thought a moment. "You know, I gotta take back that tough part. She is tough. Seeing her walking like that you wouldn't know she was using a walker two days ago." He nodded toward the alcove. "Let's get that coffee."

When Eleanor saw Peter get off the elevator a pleasant warmth came over her. He was familiar, and nicely so. He reminded her of David Niven: tall, straight bearing and sophisticated appearance. David Niven was her one true love. All those movies she had gone to, just because he had been in them. It was a very long time ago, but the emotion was still with her. Her life had been filled with men who were a disappointment, and David Niven had helped her get through all that. He reminded her that there was a civilized man out there in the world. She could always depend on David Niven. Silly, she thought, and smiled to herself.

Benny led Peter to an alcove off the lobby where there were some stuffed chairs, cocktail tables, a couple of regular tables and chairs, and an urn of coffee with the cups and fixings. One wall was glass, floor to ceiling, overlooking the swimming pool and the lake beyond. There were two women sitting at one of the tables. "They set up the pot here every morning and afternoon for people like me who can't function without caffeine." He shrugged helplessly. "It's what keeps the old brain clear and heart ticking."

"I am no longer able to drink it straight. The medical people have told me that caffeine is not good for my heart," Peter said and stepped over to the urn marked DECAF where he put together a cup of coffee with milk and two cubes of sugar. Benny poured himself a cup from the other urn. "Well, at seventy-three my heart needs all the kick it can get. I drink mine black so I get the caffeine undiluted." Benny led him over to the table where two women were seated.

"This is our welcoming committee," Benny said. "Eleanor Carter and Betty Jablonski, this is Peter Benington."

Peter smiled and gave a slight bow to the women. "Delighted to meet you both."

"Oh, he's so English," Betty Jablonski said, her voice tiny and fragile, her black eyes alive with joy. She was fluttering with excitement. She was a dumpy little woman with her hair dyed black to match her black button eyes, and wearing a dress with tiny flowers. There was a strand of diamonds around her neck. "Marjorie had said you were so polite, like royalty. Are you royalty?"

"No," he smiled, his eyes catching notice of the necklace. "I'm not really English, either. I was born in America, but raised in England. The accent was honed in Oxford. I'm afraid time has done little to Americanize it."

"Well, don't apologize," Eleanor said, her voice smooth and confident, a woman in control. She gave him a knowing smile, her light blue eyes were cool and, searching his, seemed to peer into his mind, reading it and exposing his secrets. "The accent suits you very well." An attractive woman, she sat upright with a sense of regal bearing. Her brown hair was informally coiffed and ended just above her shoulders. There was a brightly colored scarf draped around her neck and pinned with a brooch on the left shoulder over her white blouse. It was the brooch that caught Peter's eye. A small oval of blue, surrounded by tiny diamonds, with a larger diamond mounted in the center of the blue stone. Eleanor was aware of where Peter's eyes were, and her knowing smile widened.

"Does everyone wear their diamonds when they greet a new resident?" Peter said. He sat in the chair next to Eleanor, and set his cup of coffee on the table. Benny sat in the chair opposite.

"Marjorie said you knew all about jewelry," Betty said. She was bubbling with excitement. "Something about your work. You must tell us about it."

"Marjorie was wearing her diamond necklace for you," Eleanor said. "She left before you came down. She wasn't feeling well."

"I think it's the flu that's going around," Betty jumped in. "She complained that breakfast tasted funny. You know how the flu affects how things taste. And she looked pale, and sweaty."

"I met her in the hall upstairs," Peter said. "And she did not look well." He took a sip of his coffee, then pulled back from the cup and frowned. "What the devil?" A sugar cube was floating on the surface of the coffee. "The cube doesn't seem to want to dissolve?' He removed it with his fingers, and squeezed the cube. It squeezed like a sponge. He looked up to the others for an explanation. Benny suddenly laughed aloud. Betty giggled, and Eleanor smiled.

"Welcome to Coral Sands, the fun house of Florida," Eleanor said. "You have been victimized by our resident practical joker. Outside society is plagued by mad bombers. We have a mad joker."

Peter still looked puzzled. What sort of place had he moved into?

"Nobody knows who is doing it," Eleanor said. Benny was still laughing too hard to speak. "But you have to admit it does break up the monotony."

"This is most confusing," Peter said. Confused, he knew was the wrong word. Crazy was a better choice, but he didn't want to upset the others at the table.

"Oh"—Betty was still giggling—"You'll get used to it. And it is such nice fun sometimes. We all need a laugh once in a while." She looked over at Benny, who was getting himself under control. "Isn't that right, Benny?"

Benny was choking on his own laughter. "I hope they never catch the guy. Brings a little excitement in the day."

Peter leaned back, and sighed. "I guess I'll have to be more careful." He removed a gold cigarette case from his shirt pocket, opened it, and offered a cigarette to everyone at the table.

"Oh, no," Betty said, holding her hand up in defense, her nose wrinkling in distaste. "But you go ahead. It's okay."

Eleanor took one. "English?" she said.

"No I'm afraid, American. Benson & Hedges." He offered one to Benny who shook his head no.

"But it sounds English," Betty said. Everything she said seemed to gush out in bubbly, excited tones.

Peter put a cigarette in his mouth, closed the case, then snapped a flame on the lighter mounted on the end of the case, and lit Eleanor's cigarette and his own. He released a stream of smoke, then turned to Eleanor. "So what does this welcoming committee actually do?"

"Well," Eleanor said, "we try to make you feel at

home." She raised her eyebrow suggestively. "We introduce you around, and we answer any questions you may have."

Peter's eyes met Eleanor's, and he smiled playfully. "I do come from a home with strange customs."

It was Eleanor's turn to flirt. "You must tell me about them, and we'll see what we can do to create a homey atmosphere for you."

Betty giggled. "You are a wicked man. Marjorie should have warned us."

"I have one question," Peter said. "I did not receive a key to the door to my apartment. Where may I get one?"

"We leave the doors unlocked," Benny said. "The only people who would really steal anything are the maids, and they already have keys. Besides, if something happened to you, we could get in and help you without waiting for somebody from the office to find a key for the door. With heart attacks you got to get help as fast as possible."

Peter nodded. "Seems reasonable enough."

"They'll be serving lunch soon," Benny said. "Why don't I give you the penny tour of the joint, and then we can chat over lunch?"

Betty Jablonski was disappointed. "But there are so many questions we want to ask of Peter."

"Write 'em down, and we'll do it over lunch." Benny pushed his chair back and stood up. "What do you say, Peter? Ready to meet a few more people?"

Peter shrugged. "It must be done. Why not get it over with now?" He stood and turned to the ladies. "If you will excuse me. I look forward to joining you both at lunch."

Betty Jablonski's shoulders hunched tightly as if she had a chill, and her face squeezed with pleasure. "Oh, I just love the way you talk." Then she waved her hand at Benny.

"Be sure you introduce him to Tweedledee and Tweed-ledum."

Peter followed Benny into the lobby. He was bewildered. *What sort of place is this?* he thought. *A drunk wandering down the hall in her nightgown, a clown dashing through the lobby, a mad practical joker on the loose, and now Tweedledee and Tweedledum? Sounds more like an asylum than a retirement residence. And I've only been out of my room an hour.*

"I'll give you a quick tour of the activities rooms," Benny said, and led off down the hall off the lobby.

Peter shook his head and followed.

Marjorie Boyd had undressed, taken some aspirin and a bicarbonate of soda to settle her stomach, and crawled into bed. But the pain hadn't gone away. It grew in short staggering spurts that left her breathless. Her body and the bedclothes were wet, drenched with perspiration, her hair matted to her head. The pains came and went, each coming more severe. The last, a hot stabbing that caused her to cry out.

She'd never felt anything like this before except maybe in childbirth. And like childbirth, the muscles in her abdomen tightened with each spasm of pain. She struggled out of bed, got the heating pad from the drawer of the night table, plugged it in, and placed the pad on her stomach. The heat felt good, a soothing warmth that spread deeper into her body. And it took the sharp edges off the pains.

The relief was temporary. *God,* she thought. *What the hell is wrong with me?* The sweat ran down her face and off her body, her nightgown soaked, sticking to her. She couldn't think clearly around the pain. She tried to think of what she could do, but no thoughts were clear. Her mind was a jumble of heavy fatigue, and sharp points of pain.

Her body twisting and convulsing. Harder and harder. *Oh, God, make it stop.*

The pain grew like a storm racing in from the horizon. And then it exploded over her, sending solid rods of hot pain into her brain, and throwing her body in terrible writhing spasms.

"Oh, help me," she whimpered through clenched teeth, crying with the pain, tears running with the perspiration on her face. The spasms grabbed her like giant fists, tightening her body and throwing it around on the bed. She fell to the floor, convulsing with the fire inside her, arms and legs flailing about, slamming against the floor. Her teeth crashed together as she bit hard against the pain, and a tooth broke off. Her mind filled with an awful fear. Then the pain grew like a hot fireball that moved to overwhelm her, her heart stumbling in its effort, her breathing no longer possible to control.

CHAPTER

3

"It is for my mother," the Cuban said. His voice was soft and his tone was even, like warm oil on velvet.

Jessie Cummings didn't like the man. He gave her a slimy feeling that made her skin crawl. He was sitting in the chair by her desk. Maybe it was the dark glasses. Maybe his unemotional manner. She couldn't figure it out. Not that she tried very hard. There are some people you didn't like on sight, and that's it. And it had nothing to do with business.

"She is advancing in years," the Cuban said, "and I would like for her to have a nice place to live where she will be taken care of and have friends."

"Well, Mr. Vasquez," Jessie said, "I'm sure you have researched us before you came, and found that we have an excellent reputation. We've been in operation for over twenty years without any problems. We pride ourselves on being like one large family here. Our staff are pleasant, and are chosen for the ability to work with the elderly. You may speak with any of our residents, and get their view, if you wish."

"There was a clown in the lobby?"

"Yes," Jessie smiled. "One of our residents does charity work entertaining children at the hospital. The kids love her clowning around with them." The pun had no effect on him. She wasn't surprised.

"How long have you worked here?" he said.

"Ten years," she smiled. "And I love my job."

He nodded without emotion. "You do not have doctors, I know."

"We are not a nursing home, Mr. Vasquez. We supply retirees with a place where they can meet others, and enjoy activities, without the burden of all the little nuisances of life. Our dining room produces three meals a day, and each apartment has its own efficiency kitchen. This is their home. There is, however, a paramedic on duty during the night. We have an arrangement with the Rescue Squad where they can moonlight for some extra money. It seems that most emergencies happen at night. So, we feel confident that there is a competent person on hand to administer emergency treatment while waiting for the Rescue Squad to arrive. Our regular staff are trained in first aid for the same reason." Then she frowned at him. "Does your mother need medical care?"

"No. She is solid peasant ancestry. Healthy as horse."

"Well, before I take you on a tour of the Home, we must discuss the costs of living here."

"I know your fees. Three thousand a month. I am correct?"

"Plus telephone," Jessie said, "the laundry, and the dining room service, which we estimate at around seven hundred a month more."

"That is not a problem, I think. I am concern about her security, her possessions."

"Well, we can't guarantee anything. But, I can tell you

we haven't had any thefts in years." Except for some silverware, she thought. "And we have safe-deposit boxes, like those in the banks, where she can keep her valuables, if she wishes. Again, we accept no responsibility. We will give her the only keys. Should she lose them, we would have to replace the lock."

"That is satisfactory," he said. "Is the owner, Mr. Jacobson, in today?"

"No. Mr. Jacobson doesn't have an office in the Home. He stops by on occasion. But other than those visits, we rarely see him. He leaves the management of the Home to me."

"I see."

"Are there any other questions?"

"For now, I must say, no."

"Then," she said, smiling and rising to her feet, "let me show you around."

The Cuban rose to his feet. "Is a nice place. Maybe I buy it. And you work for me."

"I don't think it's for sale," she said.

The Cuban moved his mouth into a sly smile.

"Okay," Benny said. "I've showed you the rec room, the pool room, the exercise room, the card room, and the activities room. Now, there are two people you gotta meet." Benny pushed open the glass door leading out to the concrete deck and swimming pool.

Peter followed. He squinted in the sunlight. He stopped, looked around, and took in a long satisfying breath. Now there were only a few cloud smears off in the distance. Above where he stood, the sky was an endless bright blue. The surface of the lake made small ripples in the light breeze. The trees on the far shore of the lake, the water, the very air was sharp and brilliant. Beyond the swimming pool there was a gazebo by the edge of the lake. It was made of a wood that had gone dark and weathered. There were a few chairs in the gazebo. Benny moved toward the gazebo. Peter walked after him. Two men sat in the chairs looking out at the lake and at the trees and shrubbery on the other side.

One of the men wore thin sneakers, dark pants and a gray T-shirt that read WE'RE OFF OUR ROCKERS on the back. The hat he wore looked like the peaked cap of a sea captain, except this one, though still white, was worn, and hung on the head like a limp rag. Too many washings, too much wear. He looked much the same as his hat—too much wear. His skin was nut tough and wrinkled everywhere. Eighty if a day. He was short and very thin, his back bent just a bit. He sat in the chair with his legs crossed and his arms up, his hands tucked behind his head. Reflector sunglasses covered his eyes.

The other man was as old, but he wore no hat, and his skin was more fair and less wrinkled. His gray hair was long and thin and flew everywhere in the breeze. Not enough hair to hold each strand in place. He didn't much care how his hair looked. He was beyond trying to impress anyone. He wore a sport shirt that was a spectacle of color once, but the colors had faded over time to muted pastels. The tan cotton pants he'd had for years, and they looked it. He sported a new pair of white designer sneakers. He, too, was thin, but tall to almost gangly. He was stretched out; his long legs, reaching far out from the chair, were crossed at the ankles. His hands were folded on his chest. He, too, wore sunglasses.

"Suppose to go up into the eighties today," Sailor Hat said. He spoke to the lake. Neither man looked at the other. They focused their attention on the lake and world beyond.

"I'm up in the eighties everyday," Gray Hair said, and chuckled at his little joke.

"You talking about your IQ?" Sailor Hat said.

"Hey, guys," Benny said as he came up behind the two men. They turned their heads to look at him over their shoulders. "We got a new resident I want you to meet." Peter stepped next to Benny, and nodded politely. The two men eyed Peter up and down without saying a word. "This is Peter Benington." Then Benny said to Peter, "Henry Hendersen and Harry Hollis. The 4H Club."

"Good to make your acquaintance gentlemen," Peter said.

The two men nodded. "We're the 4H Club, and this"— Gray Hair said, indicating the building of apartments—"is where we keep our best animal specimens."

Sailor Hat chuckled. "Easy to see our best specimens are a pretty sorry lot."

"Well, we don't have much to work with," Gray Hair said.

"A *new* resident," Sailor Hat said, stressing the word "new." Then to Gray Hair, "He look new to you?"

Gray Hair looked carefully at Peter, then shook his head. "They ain't making 'new' like they used to. Look at all them wrinkles."

"That's it. Maybe he needs a little ironing, then he'd look new. Now, he looks pretty used."

"Could be the hair, too. They'd have to give him more hair. Sorta has a large scalp."

"I remember when I had a full head of hair," Sailor Hat said.

Gray Hair looked at him. "Nobody's got that good a memory."

Benny and Peter walked away from the two men who were still bantering about hair.

"Tweedledee and Tweedledum," Benny said, nodding with his head in the direction of the two men. "Now you know why we call them that."

"Well, they certainly are a strange lot," Peter said.

"Takes all kinds," Benny said with a shrug of his shoulders. "Let's go eat."

They walked back through the glass doors into the lobby. "You play poker?" Benny said. " 'Cause we got an empty chair at the game tonight if you're interested. Nothing big. Nickel, dime."

"I have held my own with the cards," Peter said.

Benny grinned. "Just the kind of player we skin alive. My room—208."

Benny had taken two steps into the lobby and was turning in the direction of the dining room when he heard someone calling him. He turned toward the front desk.

"Benny!" It was Georgie Allan. Twelve years old and into the gawky stage, all arms and legs.

Benny waved, and turned toward the kid. Over his shoulder he said to Peter, "Marjorie's grandson. Comes by a lot to visit her. Nice kid." Peter followed Benny to the desk.

"Hi, Georgie," Benny said. "Come by to visit your grandma?"

"Yeah," Georgie said. "I brought this." He raised his hand holding a paper bag. "Some of Mom's bread pudding from last night. Mom sent it over. Grandma ate a lot of it. Grandma said to me it was something she couldn't resist, 'cause Mom puts a lot of raisins in it. But it made her a little sick. She ate too much she said."

Benny smiled. "Well, she still wasn't feeling good this morning. She's up in her room."

Georgie shrugged. "Grace says she doesn't answer the phone."

Benny looked over at Grace behind the desk. Grace shrugged again. "I let it ring. No answer." Then Grace looked at Peter. Her eyes sparkled at him, and she smiled.

"Mr. Benington. Susan left a message that you had arrived last night. Everything okay?"

Benny said to Peter, "Grace has been here longer than me." Then, still talking to Peter, he looked over at Grace and smiled. "And she hasn't aged a day. I've done the growing old for both of us." Looking back to Peter, Benny continued, "Grace is a good person to know. She knows everything going on in this place."

"And you know everyone," Grace said to Benny. Then to Peter, "We call him the Mayor of Coral Sands."

"Nice to meet you, Grace," Peter said. He gave her his warm, gracious smile.

"Any problems, questions, don't hesitate to ask me," she said, clearly extending an invitation of an intimate nature.

Peter smiled once more at Grace. "Thank you."

Jessie Cummings came out of the open door behind Grace. "I overheard the conversation." She smiled at Peter and stepped to the counter. She smiled at Benny, and then said to Peter, "Welcome to Coral Sands. I hope your stay lives up to your expectations. I see our honorary mayor has taken you in hand. I'm sure he can answer most of your questions. One of these days I'm going to be forced to put him on the payroll. Is everything all right with your apartment? We do our best to clean up and correct any problems before someone checks in."

Peter turned his suave smile on Jessie Cummings. "Everything is superb."

"Well," she said, "my office door is always open." She smiled once again, then went back into her office.

He watched her walk away. Charming woman, Peter thought with a little lust, then turned to Georgie Allan. "If your grandmother doesn't answer the phone, she may be resting."

"Oh, Georgie," Benny said, "this here is Peter Benington. A new resident, and a friend of your grandma's."

Georgie looked up at Peter. "Pleased to meet you."

"My pleasure," Peter said. "When I saw your grandmother this morning she said she was going to rest for a little while."

"Well, maybe you can bring this to her?" Georgie held out the paper bag. "Tell her my mom sent it over."

"What say we all go give it to her?" Benny asked. "Seeing you'll make her feel better."

"Okay." Georgie shrugged. He and Peter followed Benny across the lobby to the elevator.

"How did your grandma's visit go last night?" Benny said as they climbed into the elevator.

"Not too good," Georgie said. "Her and Mom were kinda stiff."

"Yeah, well, you got to give them things time. Not easy for two people, who had such trouble between them, to put it behind them."

"Yeah, I guess. But I'd really like it if they could. Mom and Grandma haven't gotten along since I can remember."

"Last month, when I met your grandmother," Peter said, "she spoke well of your mother, and you. She said she was very proud of you both."

Benny said, "Let this be a lesson to you, Georgie. When you get married, have more than one kid. That way, if you don't get along with one of them, you'll still have friends in the others."

"Mom and Grandma have been fighting for so long, I don't think they remember why. Last night there was a time when Mom said something and I thought they were going to start hollering at each other. But Dad said something, and they held it in." Georgie shrugged. "I think they stopped because of me being there."

They got off the elevator at the third floor, and started down the hall.

"I think the problem is money," Georgie said.

"What makes you think that?" Benny said.

"Well, Mom and Dad fight a lot, and it's always about money." He shrugged. "Sometimes Grandma's name comes up when they fight. I think it's about Grandma's money."

Everything is about money, Peter thought.

"Mom wants Grandma to move in with us. She says it cost too much money for Grandma to stay here. She says they're cheating Grandma out of her money here. I want Grandma to move in with us, too. It would be fun having her around."

Benny said, "Your Grandma would like to have you around more, too. But it ain't easy for your grandma to be dependent on your mother. Not yet, anyway."

"Well," Georgie said, "that's what they started talking about when Dad made them stop."

They stopped outside room 312, and Benny knocked lightly on the door. "Marjorie, it's Benny. Georgie's here. Come to cheer you up. You okay in there?"

No sound came from inside the apartment. They looked at one another, waiting for someone to make a decision.

"I'll go in and see if she's okay," Benny said, and opened the door. "You guys wait here a minute." Benny stepped inside the apartment and partially closed the door.

"Maybe I should just leave the bread pudding and come back later?" Georgie asked of Peter.

Peter nodded in reassurance. "We ought to see what she says, first. Sometimes when people are not feeling well, a visitor is just what they need."

Benny came out, and his expression was stiff and shadowed. "Georgie, I think it's better you wait downstairs for a minute. Your grandma ain't ready to see you.''

"Well, I'll just leave this for her, and come back later.''
He held out the brown paper bag.

"I'll take this for her,'' Benny said, and took the bag
from Georgie. "But you go downstairs and wait in the
lobby for me, okay?''

Georgie shrugged, puzzled. "Okay.''

"Don't go home, now. You wait for me.''

"All right, I'll wait downstairs.'' Georgie hesitated, confused, a question on his face. Then he shrugged, turned,
and headed back toward the elevator.

"What appears to be the problem, Benny?'' Peter said
in a low voice. "Is she all right?''

"She's dead.''

Peter frowned in disbelief. "Dead?'' The word repeated
in his head. Dead. She hadn't looked sick enough to be
dead.

"And not a pretty sight, either. I didn't want the kid to
see her like that. C'mon.'' Benny went back inside the
apartment, and Peter followed.

"There,'' he said, pointing to the bedroom.

Peter walked into the bedroom while Benny got on the
phone and called downstairs to the office. The smell twisted
Peter's stomach immediately, urine and excrement. Peter
stared at the body of the woman he had spoken to only a
short time before. The sight of her grabbed him by the
throat. She looked broken, her body twisted and her arms
and legs at all angles. He had difficulty recognizing the
body as Marjorie. "God,'' he said. "How did this happen?''

"Comes with being old. Friends die a lot,'' Benny said
from the other room.

"So violently?'' Peter stepped back into the living room,
away from the ugly sight and the foul smell. His stomach

was a tight knot, and he thought he would vomit.

Benny was hanging up the phone. "Death comes in a lot of ways. Some of them not pretty." He saw the look on Peter's face. "Take a glass of cold water from the fridge. It'll help settle your stomach."

"But she hadn't looked sick enough to . . . to die?" He took the plastic bottle of water from the refrigerator, and poured himself a glass. He took it in large gulps, the cold like a weight moving down to his stomach.

Benny shrugged. "Look, we can't help her now. They'll be coming here any minute to lock up the apartment until a doctor comes. We got to think about that kid downstairs. We got to break this to him."

"Damn," Peter said.

When they got off the elevator in the lobby, Georgie was sitting on a sofa, looking a little bored. Until he spotted Benny and Peter. Then he looked worried.

"What's the matter with Grandma?" Georgie asked when they came up to him.

Benny sat down next to Georgie, and spoke in a soft low tone. "There's no easy way to say this, Georgie. . . . She's not with us anymore." Georgie's eyes grew wide. "She had some sort of an attack. She went quickly and quietly." Everyone wants to go quickly and quietly, Benny thought. "I'm sorry," he said. Peter thought it a bizarre scene, this skinny old man in a baseball cap telling the boy that his grandmother had died.

Georgie said nothing. He just looked at Benny, searching his face for some answer, some reason, some sense in all this. The silence hung like a heavy weight around them. Then Benny saw the kid's eyes begin to water. "C'mon, Georgie," he said gently. "We'll take you home." Benny looked up to Peter. Peter nodded.

Georgie stood up, swallowed hard, and said in a voice brittle with sadness, "Okay."

Benny got up and the three of them went outside to the parking area. Benny led them to a 1978 Mercury Marquis that, under the dust, was a faded yellow. With a movement of his head, Benny indicated to Peter the bicycle leaning next to the entrance to Coral Sands. While Benny put Georgie in the car, Peter brought over the bicycle, and helped Benny put it in the trunk, using a tie-down to keep the trunk lid in place.

They drove in silence. Peter sat in the back and looked at the boy sitting in the front next to Benny. He wanted to say something to the kid to soothe him, to help him cope with the pain. But there were no words to fill such a time. It took a little more than ten minutes to reach Georgie's pink stucco home. Peter saw by its size that it was not the house of a laborer. Benny pulled the car into the driveway, next to the gray Mercedes parked to one side.

"Dad's home," Georgie said. There was no emotion in his voice.

"I'm sure he knows already," Benny said. Answering the question Georgie had not spoken.

They got out of the car and walked Georgie up to the front door and into the house. It was cool inside. Richard Allan came into the foyer to greet them. He was a good-looking man in his forties, with dark hair and a clean look. A man behind a desk, not one from the factory floor, Peter thought. Richard Allan met Benny's gaze. "Thank you, Benny, for bringing Georgie home." He put his arm around Georgie's shoulders. Georgie looked to be in shock, and did not respond to his father's arm on his shoulders. "Madeliene phoned me at work, right after Mrs. Cummings called from the home. She's in the other room now, talking to . . ."

"I told her not to stay in that place!" Madeliene was shouting as she came into the foyer. There was anger and pain in her face. She spotted Benny and Peter. She turned on Benny. "I told her," she said to Benny. "That place was not good for her. She belonged here with us. I told her. I told her a hundred times. What was she thinking, not wanting to live here?" The words rushed out of her in a fury. "Can you tell me why she didn't want to stay with us? Can you!"

Richard Allan moved to his wife, and gently pulled her back. "Easy, Maddie. Easy." He held her to him.

She looked up at him, her body stiff, resisting him. "How could they do this to her? They killed her, I'm sure. Took all her money, then killed her. I never liked that place. I never liked that bitch that runs the place. Never. They're probably stealing her things right now. She should have stayed with us. Why didn't she, Richard. Why?"

Benny nudged Peter, and they quietly left the house.

During the drive back Peter was in shock. All he could think of was: What a day! Not at all like he had expected. God, not at all. It was like going to a movie expecting a love story and getting the comedy of the Three Stooges, and the horror of Frankenstein. Poor, dear Marjorie. And the day wasn't over yet.

"Some of the plates are missing." Manuel was standing in the doorway to Jessie Cummings's office.

"Not now, Manuel," Jessie said, exasperated. Some days were real trouble. And this was turning out to be one of them. "I've got bigger problems than dishes." She was going through a drawer in the file cabinet, her back to him.

"Bigger than people not being able to eat?"

"They'll eat, Manuel. Don't worry."

"We could put the food in their hands, maybe. Or drop it on the table in front of them. Tell them to eat with their hands like in India. Or . . ."

She turned on him. "Manuel, get out of here! I've got to deal with the police in a few minutes. That's more important right now!" She turned back to the file cabinet.

"The police! This is about the spoons?"

"God, Manuel, I don't have time for this." Then to herself, "Where the hell is that file?"

"You think I am suspect in this?"

"Manuel." Her shoulders sagged in surrender. "It is not about the spoons, or the dishes. Mrs. Boyd died this morning. Her bitchy daughter came in an hour ago to clear out her mother's things. She didn't waste any time, that one. Relatives are like vultures sometimes. In the safe-deposit box for Mrs. Boyd there was jewelry missing. Expensive jewelry, Manuel. And now the police are coming to investigate. Okay?'' Then she shouted past Manuel, ''Grace, you got a hold of the attorney yet!''

''No,'' Grace hollered back. ''I left another message at his office.''

''Like cops,'' Jessie said under her breath. ''They're never around when you need them.'' Then louder, ''Grace, what about Jacobson? You get him yet?''

''No,'' Grace shouted. ''Left a message on his machine.''

''Shit,'' Jessie said to herself. Then she looked at Manuel. ''Anything else?''

''No.'' He gave her an exaggerated shrug. ''I see you are busy now. I will come back later, if that is okay?''

''Fine, Manuel. Later.''

He nodded and left.

She went back to digging in the file drawer. ''Damn, Marjorie Boyd, where are you?'' Then she took hold of a file folder. ''Gotcha!'' She pulled it out, dropped it on her desk, and dropped herself in the chair.

Grace appeared in the doorway. ''The arrangements have been made for the mourners' lunch tomorrow.''

''Good,'' Jessie Cummings said.

Grace continued, ''And the Allans are back, and there's a policeman in uniform, and a detective with them.'' She looked at the business card in her hand. ''A detective Ralph Ardley.''

Jessie Cummings threw her hands over her face. ''Oh, God.'' She let out a huge sigh, and dropped her hands. ''Okay, let's get this over with.''

•   •   •

"I find it difficult to accept that Marjorie is dead," Peter said.

Benny said, "It ain't ever easy. But when you're my age, you know you ain't too far from the end. The days you got left mean a lot more."

"Getting old means your friends are old," Eleanor said, "and more likely to die at any time. That's not a nice arrangement."

"I told Marjorie there would be trouble," Betty was saying. "Eugene had warned me only last week. He told me to make sure I told Marjorie to be careful. He said it was not a good time for her."

"Well," Benny said, "he wasn't exaggerating."

The four of them were sitting outside by the swimming pool. They sat at a table in the shade under the large awning that ran along one wall. They were grouped around one side of the table so they could see the view. It was after four. Peter had had no stomach for eating when they had returned from Georgie Allan's house. Now, he and the others were sipping at glasses of iced tea.

"Who is Eugene?" Peter asked. Eleanor gave him a hard frown. But it was too late to take the question back.

"Oh," Betty smiled sweetly, "Eugene is my husband. I speak with him a lot. And when he tells me something, he is never wrong. Is he Eleanor?"

"No, he isn't. He is uncanny."

"I think he talks too much, myself," Benny said and sipped at his drink. Eleanor gave him a poke with her elbow. "Oow!" he said. "That hurt. You could break a rib. You got real sharp elbows."

"They are my best weapons," Eleanor said. Her expression was stern.

"Oh, it's all right, Eleanor," Betty said. "Benny's not

a believer. I know that.'' Then she turned to Peter. ''Do you believe in talking with the spirits?''

Peter swallowed hard at the iced tea in his mouth, and tried to keep his expression neutral. ''Spirits?'' he said, though he knew what she meant. Eleanor turned her stern look on him, warning him he was on dangerous ground.

''The dead. Those who have passed on to the other side,'' Betty said. ''You see, Eugene has been dead for eight years now. But I still talk with him. He helps me every chance he can. He is such a darling man.''

Uh oh, Peter thought. *Here we go again.* Eleanor was watching him very carefully. ''Well, I have never had reasons to believe otherwise.'' He hoped that came out right.

Eleanor jumped in to change the subject. ''Marjorie's daughter is saying that Marjorie's jewelry was stolen.'' They turned their attention to her. ''I was talking to Grace a little while ago. The list of jewelry that her daughter had did not match what was in the safe-deposit box. Grace said the daughter claimed there was over fifty thousand dollars worth of jewelry that was missing. And she accused Jessie of stealing it. Bad news that daughter of Marjorie's. Imagine showing up a couple of hours after her mother is dead to get the woman's jewelry? What kind of person is that?''

''A relative,'' Benny said, ''who is an heir. Money does that. The cops showed up a few minutes ago,'' Benny said. ''I saw them come into the lobby with Marjorie's daughter and son-in-law.''

The police! Peter thought. *God, is this day never going to end?*

''Now, Maddie, take it easy,'' Richard Allan said.

''Don't stick up for them.'' She bit the words at him, her face set in a hard expression. ''This is the list that I had, and there was a copy in Mom's safe-deposit box. On it is all the jewelry she had in the box. And now much of it is gone! They stole it." With a flash of her eyes and a nod, she indicated Jessie Cummings. "What else could have happened to it?"

"We don't have a key to the box," Jessie Cummings said. "And here"—she pulled a sheet of paper from the file folder in her hand—"is the paper Mrs. Boyd signed, accepting full responsibility for the contents of the safe-deposit box."

Madeliene Allan, in a rage, put her face right in Jessie Cummings's face, and spit the words at her. "Oh, all wrapped up nice and tight. But how do we know you don't have a key? How hard was it to make a duplicate before you turned the key over to my mother? What a nice racket you've got. Well, I'm not going to let you get away with it!"

Jessie Cummings wanted nothing else than to punch Madeliene Allan in the face. Instead, she took a deep breath to push back her anger. "This sort of talk will not resolve anything." *Dear God, save me from the grieving relatives who inherit the money.*

"Oh yes, it will. I'll . . ."

"Excuse me, Mrs. Allan," Detective Ardley said, putting a hand up to quiet things. His voice was like fine gravel. "Please let me ask a few questions."

Madeliene bit her lip and stepped back.

The detective turned to Jessie. He was a big man with a sweat-stained white shirt, a bulging waist, and a thick head of gray hair. "Mrs. Cummings, would there . . ."

"It's Ms.," Jessie said.

She saw his gray eyes go cold for a moment. "Ms. Cummings." He nodded and then continued in an even tone, apparently a man used to being patient. "Would there be any duplicate keys around? Would anyone on the staff have a key?''

"No. We have two keys made for each safe-deposit box. And both keys are given to the owner of the box. In this case, to Mrs. Boyd.''

"And who holds these two keys before the box is rented?''

"The box is actually purchased by the resident for the price of installing the lock. The box is a service we extend to the residents without charge. And I hold the two keys until someone buys the box.''

"And that's when she makes herself a copy!'' Madeliene said, in a knowing snarl.

"Maddie,'' Richard Allan said calmly, "let the man do his job.''

Madeliene let out an exasperated sigh and pulled herself back.

Detective Ardley turned to Madeliene and Richard. He wasn't sure a crime had been committed. Old people have lousy memories, and they do things that are strange. He wouldn't be a bit surprised if the old woman took the jewels and buried them in the backyard because she was afraid some imaginary thief was after them. Wouldn't be the first time. Now, he wanted to defuse this situation quickly, before Mrs. Allan blew up, and things got out of hand. Best he could do was go through the motions, delay this a few days until these people cooled off, and let the whole thing drop. "What I can do is to check to see if the box was tampered with and check for fingerprints. Possibly, the person who took the jewels was careless.'' Then to Jessie Cummings, "And I'd have to fingerprint your staff and the residents. See if we can exclude them.''

"All of the residents!'' Jessie said. *God, what a nightmare.*

"No," he said. "I think we can first narrow it to her close friends. And maybe anyone who is a recent resident. I think this theft happened recently. If it had happened a while ago, the woman herself would have complained. Might have happened today, after Mrs. Boyd was found dead."

"Maybe she killed her," Madeliene said. "That's it. Kill my mother, then rob the stuff from her box."

"Please," Detective Ardley said, again with the hand up. "Let's not get carried away here. One step at a time, now." He glanced over at the uniformed policeman standing to one side. The policeman looked to the heavens for help.

"Can this be done discreetly?" Jessie said. All she needed was to get everyone upset. "A lot of the people here are elderly, and they can't take too much upsetting."

With all the elderly in Sarasota he had to deal with, Ardley knew firsthand how upset they could get. He nodded. "I understand. I'll have a man over here soon to dust the box. Maybe by then you could give us a list of those people close to her, and anyone who recently arrived. You could call them into your office, and he could get their prints then. Make up any story you like." He turned back to Madeliene and Richard. "That way we could have this settled by tomorrow afternoon." And get it out of his hair quickly, so he could get back to chasing the real criminals. "And Mr. and Mrs. Allan, you will both have to be fingerprinted, since you were handling the box today. If you like you can come back to the station with me, and do that."

"That'll be fine," Richard Allan said. He was anxious to get Madeliene out of there.

"I don't think Richard touched the box," Madeliene said, with a resentful look at Richard. "He just stood off to the side and watched." Richard avoided her eyes.

"We'll take his fingerprints just in case he touched something." Detective Ardley again turned to Jessie Cummings. "I'll leave the patrolman here to see that the box is not tampered with until it can be fingerprinted."

Madeliene said, "I want an autopsy on my mother. I wouldn't put it past this woman to have killed her."

"Maddie, now stop this," Richard Allan's voice was suddenly firm. "The doctor already said it was a massive stroke."

"I don't believe the doctor!" she snapped at him. "How could he tell just by looking at her! I want that autopsy. She's not going to get away with this."

"Maddie, be reasonable," Richard said, trying to soothe her. "She was an old woman. She had diabetes, and who knows what else. These things happen."

"You don't know," she snapped back, "that she doesn't do this all the time. Kill them and steal their things."

Richard Allan rolled his eyes. "C'mon, Maddie. You're losing it. We'll talk about this later."

"I'm not going to change my mind," she stated, her face tight with determination.

Detective Ardley jumped in quickly. "Do you have any photographs of the jewelry?" *Nothing worse to deal with than an emotional woman. Have to move this along quickly.*

"No," Madeliene said. "But I know what they all looked like."

"Perhaps, while you're down at the station, you can give me a description of the missing pieces. We'll have the pawnshops look out for them. The jewelry is no good unless it can be turned into cash."

He turned to Jessie Cummings and nodded saying, "Ms. Cummings," with a little more emphasis on the Ms.

Jessie Cummings said, "Could you come back here with

the man when he takes the fingerprints? Possibly you could handle the explanations better than I.''

Detective Ardley nodded. He then escorted the Allans out of her office.

"And who was it again who died?'' It was Jacobson at the other end of the line.

"A Mrs. Marjorie Boyd,'' Jessie Cummings said. She had explained it all to him when he called. He sounded troubled, and she couldn't understand it. He had owned this residence home for many years, and people had died before. But it was true that the Home had never before been accused of stealing. Not a good mark in the publicity department. "I already spoke to Constantino, the lawyer. He said there was no way we could be held liable. But he would contact the daughter and see if he couldn't squash this before it got ugly.''

"Yes, yes. Good.'' But he didn't sound convinced. He hesitated. "You didn't . . . never mind. Who's the detective on this?''

"Ralph Ardley,'' she said.

"Ralph,'' he said, "I know him. I'll call him, and see what he says about all this.''

"He's coming back here in a little while. Do you want me to have him call you?''

"No. I'll call him tomorrow then.'' There was a moment of silence. "Jessie, are you sure it wasn't one of the staff?''

"That's not a question I can answer.'' She sure hoped it wasn't, though. She hadn't told him about the missing silverware. And she didn't think this was a good time.

"Yes. I understand. I'll call you tomorrow after I speak to Detective Ardley. You can let me know then what happens tonight.''

"There's one more thing,'' she said.

"What's that?"

She hesitated, wondering whether she should ask it, and whether he would tell her the truth. "Are you selling Coral Sands?"

"No," he said. Too quickly, she thought. "Where would you get that idea from?"

"It doesn't matter," she said. "I'll wait for your call tomorrow."

"Jessie." He hesitated. "You'll let me know if anything else happens?"

"Yes," she said, but the request puzzled her. She always kept him informed.

"Why didn't Benny join us for dinner?" Peter said. They were seated in the dining room, and he was doing his best not to wolf down the food. He hadn't eaten all day, and now he was famished.

"I think he had a more *important* engagement," Eleanor said, with a smile, stressing the word "important."

Peter frowned at her, puzzled by what she meant.

Betty giggled. "We think Benny has a serious girlfriend somewhere."

"Oh," Peter said. The thought of that skinny old man in the baseball cap going courting made Peter smile.

Betty leaned forward conspiratorially and said, "He's been so mysterious about it. He sneaks out with presents all wrapped and hidden in shopping bags. I asked him to bring her around so we could meet her. But he just grunted and said I was silly to think that he had a girlfriend. But I know. A woman can tell, can't she, Eleanor?"

Eleanor smiled. "Some men can't hide it."

Betty said, "He did say to tell you that he would be back for the card game tonight. Eight o'clock."

"I think I may avoid the card game tonight," Peter said.

"The day has been, as the children say, awesome. I may just retire early."

The waiter in a formal black outfit came to their table with a large tray of food. "Now, let's see if I get this right." He smiled, then he placed a plate of food in front of each of them. "How's that?"

"Perfect, Chris." Eleanor gave him a friendly smile. Then to Peter, "Peter, I want you to meet Chris Lassiter. He's new with us." She turned to the waiter. "What is it? A month?"

"Yes. And from what I hear from Carlos, it'll be a month or so more."

"Oh, really? Carlos is not doing well?" Eleanor said, then to Peter, "Carlos has been a waiter here for three years. Then a short while ago, he had an accident."

"Smashed up his leg on a motorcycle." Chris shook his head slowly, letting everyone see how bad it was. "He asked me to hold his job for him until he's on his feet again. I'm a friend of his, and I was between jobs. So, here I am. And I can see why Carlos doesn't want to lose this job. It's really nice working here." He looked around the table. "Can I get you anything else?"

They all shook their heads.

Chris nodded to Peter. "Nice meeting you, sir."

"Good to meet you, too, young man." Then after Chris had left, Peter turned to Eleanor. "Are you friendly with all the help?"

She smiled at him. "They're like family here."

"They're nice people," Betty said. Then, "Oh, there's Mr. Petersen! I wonder who he is today?" She called out, "Mr. Petersen! Mr. Petersen!"

Peter looked around to see who she was calling to. A thin, fragile-looking man, bald, with a sparse fringe of gray hair around the sides of his head, looked over at them. He was standing by a table filled with diners. At first he looked puzzled, as if he wasn't sure Betty was calling him.

"You! Yes, you!" she said, and waved him over.

He smiled and nodded, and came toward their table. He wore eyeglasses that were small and round, and encased in wire frames.

Betty leaned in and said in a low voice, "I never know who to call him." She smiled and shrugged like a little girl unable to contain her excitement.

"Hello, hello, my friends," the man said, and took Betty's hand and kissed it.

"We'd like you to meet a new resident," Betty said. She pointed to Peter. "This is Peter Benington."

"How do you do, Peter Benington." He extended his hand, and Peter took it. "Henny Youngman. Did you know cannibals don't eat clowns, because they taste funny? I had a terrible night last night in my hotel. There was a woman banging on the door of my hotel room all night long until I finally let her out."

"Please, Mr. Youngman." Eleanor jumped in, and put her hand on his arm.

The man turned to her. "Henny, my dear. All beautiful women call me Henny."

Eleanor dropped her eyes coquettishly. "Henny."

"That's better. It sounds so alluring when you say it."

"We would love to have you all to ourselves, but you do have obligations to the others at the dinner."

"You are right, my darling. Beautiful women like yourself are always right." He took her hand and kissed it. Then to Peter, "Nice meeting you. Sorry I can't stay. But we'll meet again, I'm sure."

Peter nodded and smiled weakly. "I'm looking forward to it." There was no shock left in him by this time.

Henny Youngman smiled. "In parting, during World

War Two a little Italian girl saved me from the war. She hid me in the cellar. It was in Cleveland." He gave the women a little wave, and headed off back to the table he had come from.

Peter looked at the women, who were smiling. *Here we go again,* Peter thought. "Please, do explain this to me?"

Betty said, "That's Mr. Petersen. A very nice man. He was some sort of engineer or scientist or something. Well . . ." She shrugged tightly. "Sometimes he thinks he's somebody else."

Peter put his hand to his forehead and rubbed his temples. Then drew the hand down over his face. He'd had enough.

"Do you have a headache?" Betty said.

He shook his head. "Thinks he's someone else?"

Betty nodded excitedly. "Isn't it so interesting?"

Peter was confused. "Is he being treated for . . . whatever it is he has that makes him think he's someone else?"

"I don't know," Betty said.

"I mean," Peter said, "shouldn't he be . . . watched?" Eleanor had been sitting silently, smiling at him. "Help me, please," he said to Eleanor. "Are there not places where such a person could receive care?"

"We care for him," Eleanor said. "It's so much nicer here than in some institution. He's harmless. And in a way, a sad old man. He's been a dull person all his life. Now, he has the chance to be someone interesting and exciting."

Betty said, "When he thinks he's Fred Astaire, he's such a good dancer. And when he's that magician fellow— Blackstone?—he is very entertaining. He does some marvelous card tricks."

"He is never a nasty character," Eleanor said. "I think it's nice he has the opportunity to act out his fantasies."

"And," Betty said, "he's so good at it. Once when he

was Sherlock Holmes he helped me find my watch. And when he was that famous chef . . . Oh, what was his name? Anyway, he gave me a wonderful recipe for pork chops that I gave to the cook, and he raved about it. I just wish he'd be a doctor sometime, because I have this problem with my neck that nobody can help me with.''

Peter sat there stunned. It had to be a dream, and he hoped it would soon be time to wake up. This place was a lunatic asylum!

Grace came over to the table. ''Mr. Benington, Jessie would like you to stop at the office for a moment, please?''

God, what now! He released a heavy sigh. ''Yes, of course.'' He stood up with an effort. ''If you will excuse me, ladies.''

''We'll wait for you for dessert,'' Betty said.

He smiled politely, then followed Grace out of the dining room.

The man in the short-sleeved white shirt sitting in the chair off to the side was obviously a cop. Peter had enough dealings with the police to recognize one in his presence. And it always made him feel apprehensive. Jessie Cummings was seated behind her desk, and there was another cop standing off to the side. Then Peter spotted the fingerprint setup on the side table.

''Mr. Benington,'' Jessie Cummings said. ''I don't want to upset you. But, well, we've had a possible theft . . .''

''Am I a suspect?'' Peter said. He kept his voice cool and polite, no indignation in the tone.

''Let me introduce myself,'' the man in the chair said. He stood up reluctantly, as if it was too much to move his weight out of the chair, and extended his hand. ''Detective Ralph Ardley.''

Peter took the man's hand and shook it.

"We are not accusing you," Detective Ardley said. He spoke easily, almost friendly. "Nor do we suspect you of anything. I'm not even sure a crime has been committed. In fact that's what I hope to prove. We are taking the prints of all of the people who may have been in contact with Mrs. Boyd, so we can exclude those prints we find that match. You see, after we have excluded all the known prints, any left over may be the criminal's. And truthfully," he lowered his tone to one of confidentiality, "I suspect we won't have any left over."

What a lot of double-talking bullshit, Peter thought. Why do police always think people are stupid?

"I hope you understand," Detective Ardley said.

"This has something to do with the stolen jewelry?" Peter said.

"Well." Detective Ardley smiled like a kid caught in a lie. "Yes, it does. I hadn't thought anyone knew about it."

"The gossip mill is hyperactive in this place," Jesse Cummings said.

"And *Ms.* Cummings," Detective Ardley said, "told me you had something to do with jewelry in your business life. Insurance investigations was it?"

He never should have told the truth in that historical profile on the application. "Yes. I had my own business, which supported the insurance industry. When there were expensive thefts of jewelry, I would manage to contact the thieves and arrange for the return of the jewelry for a fraction of what the insurance company would have to pay if the jewelry wasn't recovered."

Detective Ardley showed no visible reaction, but Peter sensed a change in the man. He was thinking now. "Interesting," he said, his voice calm and even. "How do you do that?"

"Was the jewelry insured?" Peter said, ignoring the

question, hoping it would go away. He didn't like the tone in the cop's voice. Trouble.

Detective Ardley turned to Jessie Cummings.

She shrugged. "I don't think so."

"Then I can't help you," Peter said.

"You didn't answer my question," Detective Ardley said. "How do you do that?"

"What exactly do you mean?" Peter told himself to relax. There was nothing here he had to worry about. But he wasn't convinced of that.

"How do you contact the criminals to get the jewelry back?"

"Most often they establish contact with me. They know what I do, and they know that I am able to acquire the money without additional problems."

"Interesting." Detective Ardley said the word slowly, not taking his eyes off Peter. Everything grew quiet as the two men looked at one another. "Interesting," Ardley said again. "And what about the other times, when they don't contact you?"

"I put the word out, through some people I know, that the insurance company is willing to negotiate." Peter shrugged with his eyes. "Most times they contact me after that. Only a few times was I unsuccessful."

"Interesting," Detective Ardley said. "And what a co-incidence that your first day here—a man who knows jewel thieves—and jewelry gets taken. Don't you think that's a real coincidence?"

Peter returned the man's look and said nothing. He tried to think nothing, so his thoughts wouldn't betray him. Again a silence dropped around them. It lasted for an uncomfortable time.

"Well," Ardley said suddenly, in a back-to-business

voice. "It would be appreciated if you could give us a set of prints?" He nodded in the direction of the other man who had been quietly waiting.

Peter said, "Of course."

CHAPTER
5

He felt hung over. It was after ten in the morning, and he'd been in bed since nine the previous night. But it hadn't been a restful sleep. Trouble stirred his dreams into nightmares, and threw him repeatedly awake throughout the night. Finally, his mind a mess, he got out of bed. He would have preferred to stay in bed and let the day go on without him. But there would only be another day behind this one.

He dragged himself into the kitchen—the arthritis in his hip a cranky pain—turned on the coffee maker, and swallowed a beta blocker. Two hours late for the pill, but better late than never. What surprises were awaiting him this day? God, he couldn't take many more surprises. These were supposed to be his golden years, a time of relaxation and contemplating one's navel. Trouble was supposed to be behind him. Instead, it had caught up with him, and boxed him in. Last night, after leaving Jessie Cummings's office, Peter had not gone back to the dining room. He just couldn't take anymore of that day. He went straight up to his room, cleaned up and went to bed, hoping all the craziness would go away. Things would look better after a night's sleep, he had told himself; and he had tried to believe it.

He smoked two cigarettes while he downed a cup of decaf—though he longed for the head-clearing caffeine. Then he shaved, dressed, and went down to the lobby, his stomach wound tight waiting for the shocks of the new day. There was no one in the coffee alcove, but he heard people in the dining room. Food might help unwind his stomach.

In the dining room, people crowded about a buffet table that had been laid out. In the center of the table was a picture of Marjorie in a flowered frame.

"Mourner's lunch," Eleanor said, and took his arm. She had seen him enter, and came over to him. "Jessie arranges this when someone dies in the Home. It's a way of everybody grieving, then getting on with their lives."

"Rather quickly, don't you think?" he said.

"When you consider how old everyone is, there isn't much time left to waste." She guided him over to the buffet table. "People gather, remember, and in a guilty way, are thankful they are alive." She picked up one plate for the both of them and started putting things on it. "Marjorie was a good person. I liked her. And I'll miss her. But who knows how soon after her I will go? Or any of us?"

"Morbid," he said, and added some things to the plate.

"Honest," she said. She picked up some silverware. "There aren't enough teaspoons. We'll have to share." And gave him a seductive smile. He felt himself attracted to this woman. She started toward a table near the wall. Peter went to follow and jostled a woman with his elbow.

"Sorry," he said. Eleanor stopped, and turned.

The woman looked at him and smiled innocently. She was a tiny creature, bent with osteoporosis. A tall, frail man stepped up next to her and looked at Peter. "Please forgive her," he said in a soft, patient voice. "She doesn't mean anything by it."

Peter was about to say that she hadn't done anything to apologize for when Eleanor spoke. "Mr. Walden, I'd like you to meet Peter Benington."

"Ted Walden," the man said, and delicately shook Peter's hand. "And this is my wife, Elizabeth." Then to his wife, "Say hello to Mr. Benington, dear."

The woman smiled at Peter.

Ted Walden looked at Peter with sad eyes, and shrugged his shoulders helplessly. Peter smiled softly and nodded politely to the woman.

"Nice to meet you Mr. Benington, but"—Ted Walden signaled toward his wife—"I must go."

"I understand," Peter said.

Peter and Eleanor walked to the table at the far wall and sat down. Eleanor spread out the silverware.

Peter gave Eleanor a quizzical look. "Alzheimer's," she said. Her eyes were sad as she looked over at Ted Walden guiding his smiling wife through the people toward the door to the swimming pool deck. "Really sad. She's been going downhill quickly the past few months. He's so patient with her; but, as he said to me, it's not really her. The body doesn't hold the woman he knew and loved all those years."

"Shouldn't she be in a nursing home?"

"She wouldn't get more loving care at a nursing home than she's getting from him. It would be better for his sake, maybe. But not for hers." The sigh she let out was filled with sadness. "I don't see how he can do it much longer, though."

"From what I know of the disease, it gets terribly worse," he said.

Her eyes still on Ted Walden and his wife, Eleanor nodded with sadness. "He's not strong enough to handle what's to come. And friends aren't good with chronic illness. They don't have the staying power to help him. He's pretty much on his own right now. I feel sorry for him." A depressing anger overcame the sadness. "It isn't right that society won't permit her a humane death. She's forced to waste away to nothing more than a confused and frightened animal. Not recognizing anyone, surrounded by strangers. Not understanding what's being done to her. Not knowing what is expected of her. It's so cruel. A damn shame."

They sat quietly, each with their own thoughts for a moment. Then Eleanor said, "Life's a bitch, sometimes."

They ate in silence until the terrors of life were sorted, catalogued, and put away so they could no longer dwell on them. The mind can handle only so much gloom.

Eleanor said, "You missed your dessert last night."

"Sorry. Just couldn't handle anymore of the day." With his fork, he pushed the food around on the plate. "I'm not sure I'm ready for this day either." He looked in the direction of the swimming pool deck and Ted and Elizabeth Walden. The golden years, he thought, could be hell.

"Retirement too exciting for you?" She grinned.

He turned back to her, grunted and smiled. "You might say it exactly that way."

"Not rocking chairs lined up on the front porch?" she said, picking up some food with her fork.

"Definitely not," he grinned and forked some food into his mouth.

"You rather be in the room over the garage with your kids?"

His grin broadened, "No. My son has two children and a wonderful wife. They don't need me getting in the way."

"One child?"

He nodded. "David, he's a detective on the Newark police force. That is Newark, New Jersey. My wife left me shortly after he was born."

"I'm sorry to hear that," she said.

He shrugged. "It was for the best. We married for the wrong reasons. Janice was a beautiful woman, with poise and excitement in her spirit. It was fun to be around her. When she was pregnant with David, she thought it would be interesting and exciting to have a child. When David was two she was pregnant again. She decided that being a mother and having a family wasn't what she wanted. She obtained an abortion and a divorce, and left David with me. Fortunately, it was not an ugly divorce. We both, at that point, realized it just wouldn't work. And, she had the decency not to ask for alimony, or it would have broken me." He hadn't thought about Janice in a long time. He could still see her standing on the porch with the sun shining gold in her long brown hair. She had been truly beautiful.

"You ever try again?" Eleanor broke into his thoughts.

"You mean with Janice? No," he said, his eyes still distant. "Oh, we kept in touch. She would visit occasionally. After all, she was David's mother. But the magic that brought us together had gone." And magic it was, with all the glow and mystery and wonder. He grinned, embarrassed. "Am I getting too sloppy?"

"No," Eleanor said, reaching out to him with a comforting smile. *I think you're doing just fine,* she thought.

He wanted to say that Eleanor reminded him of Janice. But he decided against it.

"Growing up, David spent a lot of time with my sister when I was traveling." He looked over at Eleanor. "You have a room over the garage to go to?"

"No. I married when I was forty-two. Matthew was sixty-one. He was a nice man, and we had some very good years. He died and that was that. I don't mean to sound cold. You can care for a person without romantic love. And Matthew was easy to care about." She sighed with exasperation. "My only problem is his brother, Mark, a real pain in the ass. For years now, he's been trying everything he can to get his hands on Matthew's money. I'll be damned if I let him get a penny, the bastard."

"Not blocking the lobby today?" The voice strong and confident. Peter looked up at the woman standing before him. She was thick and solid with dyed brown hair, and a face sagging under its wrinkles. Buried in that face were dark eyes that were glowing and alive. She smiled at him and all the wrinkles on her face fell into place. "Alice Chomseky. We met yesterday."

The clown! Peter smiled. "I didn't recognize you without your red nose."

She laughed, a full, hearty laugh. "I didn't mean to disturb you two. Just thought I'd give you a look at the real face under the red nose." She brought up her hand and wiggled her fingers in a wave. "See you around, handsome," her eyes smiling playfully at him, then she left them and headed back toward the buffet table.

He turned to grin at Eleanor. "She nearly ran me over in the lobby yesterday."

"She's a barrel of laughs in and out of her costume," Eleanor said. "Nice woman, but be careful, she speaks her mind."

"Sometimes that can be very charming in a woman." His gaze went soft, looking into Eleanor's eyes.

"Only if she says what you want to hear." She smiled back at Peter. He liked her smile.

"Do you know everyone in this place?"

"No." She smiled at the absurdity of the idea. "There are sixty-eight apartments in Coral Sands. With some of the apartments occupied by husband and wife, that makes close to a hundred people. No way do I know a hundred people. But after a while you get to know of most of them.'' She scanned the small crowd near the buffet table. ''Like Elaine Singleton,'' she said, nodding her head in the direction of a woman who looked close to emaciation. She appeared to be an unkempt woman who had just made last minute adjustments to try and look respectable before she entered the room. Even from this distance Peter could see that her eyes looked like runny egg whites. ''I know of her, but have never sat and talked with her.''

''She's the alcoholic Marjorie pointed out to me in the hall yesterday morning,'' Peter said.

Eleanor nodded, but no smile. ''Some things are best faced with a little dose of alcohol.''

''I can't take much more of this somber, depressing mood,'' Peter said.

''You through with these?'' It was Chris, the waiter. He pointed to the plate and silverware.

''Hi, Chris,'' Eleanor said gently. ''This is a first for you, isn't it?''

''Yes,'' Chris said. His eyes heavy and confused. His voice low and hesitant to go with the mood of the room. ''I just don't know how to react. I guess I don't expect people I like to die like that.''

''It comes with the game,'' Eleanor said in resignation.

''Yes, you can take the plate and the utensils,'' Peter said. Then to Eleanor, ''Would you like to go outside for awhile?''

''Love it.'' Eleanor tried a smile, and pushed back her chair.

''I toll you about the plates, yes?'' Manuel was standing in the doorway of Jessie Cummings's office.

Jessie was again at an open drawer in the file cabinet. When she heard his voice she wanted to scream. The day was turning into another bad one. "Yes, you did, Manuel," she said over her shoulder while she flipped through the file folders.

"Well, I count the cups and saucers, and they are not all there, also."

She pulled up a file folder to keep her place, then turned to Manuel, and in her nicest, most patient tone said, "Manuel, this is another bad time for me. Could we talk about this later?"

"You have so much bad times," he said.

"Yes, occasionally I do. Trouble comes in bunches, like bananas. Right now the bunch is getting bigger before my eyes."

"What do I do about feeding all the people without plates and cups and saucers? They can wait for a good time?"

She let out a sigh of patience. "Manuel, I was just told that Marcia Templeton was found dead in her apartment. I'm trying to find her folder so I can call whoever is on the notify list. I really can't deal with the problem of dishes right now. Do you understand? Please come back later."

"Another?"

She nodded wearily.

"If this happens some more," he shrugged, "we don't need no more spoons and plates. I will wait some more to see how many plates we need to feed what is left." He turned and left.

Jessie shouted through the opened door, "Grace, please get Jacobson on the phone. If you have to leave a message tell him about Marcia." She turned back to the open file drawer.

•   •   •

"What happened to Betty?" Peter said. They were walking toward the gazebo. Peter could see that Tweedledee and Tweedledum were in the same chairs as yesterday. "I didn't see her around?"

Eleanor said, "She had to go to her lawyer's this morning. Sign something, I think." Then she looked at Peter with pleading on her face. "You really shouldn't make fun of her like Benny does."

"I'll try not to," Peter said, "but you must admit that she does have a problem."

"She's a lonely old lady, who was brought up to depend on a man for everything, and the man died. She didn't even know how to make out a check. He took care of everything. He controlled her whole life. Now, the man's not in the picture, but he's the only one she could go to for advice." Eleanor shrugged. "So, she talks to him." She stopped at the side of the gazebo and leaned against its railing. Tweedledee and Tweedledum were just the other side of the railing. Eleanor met Peter's gaze. He liked it when she looked directly at him; even when there was anger in her eyes. "If she was younger, they might say she was psychic. Eugene has been pretty accurate. But she's old, so they all look at her like she's crazy. And her son is trying to get her declared incompetent, so he can get his hands on her money, and put her away someplace out of sight. Damn shame what people will do for mama's money."

"Please forgive me. I didn't know," he said.

"Yeah," she looked out at the lake. "What about the rest of the world? Will they say they're sorry?"

Peter stepped closer to her. He wanted to reach out and comfort her, but he kept his distance.

"What about Benny?" he asked, trying to change the subject. "Did he ever come back last night?"

"No." She shook her head and grinned. "And he wasn't

around this morning. She must be something special, his woman.''

Sailor Hat was wearing a T-shirt that read ROCKERS ARE A PAIN IN THE ASS on the back. He said to Gray Hair, "Saw some police around the lobby yesterday.''

Gray Hair said, "They were looking for a rapist. I gave them your name.''

"My name? My memory isn't that good. I wouldn't know how to do it anymore. Now you, that's a different story. You getting any?''

"Any what?''

"You know," Sailor Hat rolled his eyes.

"Stomach cramps? Bowel movements? What?''

"Sex, you jackass.''

"You gotta be kidding me," Gray Hair said.

"I don't know. You seem pretty tight with that Helen Wicks.''

"She's company.''

"Talk is, she's a good dancer . . . in the bedroom.''

"Go on.'' Gray Hair waved him off. "I've got arthritis.''

"Thought that gave you a stiff joint, which is what you need.''

"You ain't listening," Gray Hair grumbled. "Bouncing on the springs with my arthritis, I'd be in so much pain I wouldn't know if I was having a good time.''

Eleanor and Peter smiled at the conversation of the two men. Benny came through the doors to the deck and walked up to Eleanor and Peter. "Just heard that Marcia Templeton was found dead in her bathroom.''

"Oh, God," Eleanor said.

Peter looked in surprise. "Another?''

"Just 'cause one dies, doesn't stop the clock.''

"Hear that?'' Sailor Hat said. "Another one.''

"Dropping like flies," Gray Hair replied.

"Wonder where that expression came from?"

"What expression?"

"Dropping like flies."

"Romans probably. Sounds like it has to do with sex orgies. Or a serial rapist."

"They have zippers in Rome?"

Eleanor stood up and started walking back toward the house. Peter and Benny followed. "Those two are too old to take life, or death, seriously."

"Another one," Jacobson said. Jessie Cummings could tell he was upset.

"Yes," Jessie said.

"Is there any sign that . . . well, that it wasn't natural?"

Now, that was a question she didn't know how to take. She frowned at the telephone. "I'll have to leave that up to her doctor."

"Yes, I suppose that would be the way it's done," he said. The man definitely had something on his mind.

"Why would you think it wasn't natural?"

"I didn't think that. But I'm concerned about the reputation of Coral Sands. If there is some rumor that it wasn't a natural death, we might not be able to get people to reside there. If you know what I mean?"

"I don't think a rumor like that would have any effect on our enrollment," she said. "No matter what people think, we both know that some old people take their own lives. And it is common practice for doctors not to make an issue of it. So, I don't think you should be overly concerned. We've had deaths before. Why would you suddenly become worried about this?"

There was a moment of silence. "Maybe I'm getting old," he said. "Worrying too much. Please keep me informed."

"Good-bye, Mr. Jacobson," she said and hung up the phone. Peculiar behavior, she thought.

Detective Ardley showed up in her office a short time later. There were two policemen with him. "Afternoon, *Ms.* Cummings," he said, again stressing the "Ms."

God, what now? she thought. "Yes, Detective?"

"Sorry to bother you, but we'll need to get the fingerprints of those people that weren't around yesterday. We still have unidentified prints from the safe-deposit box. None of those we printed yesterday were on the box. Except the Allans' and Mrs. Boyd's. Mrs. Allan had said her husband hadn't touched the box, but we found his prints in it. Shows you how unreliable witnesses can be."

Jessie sighed a weary sigh. "I am very busy. Could I set you up in another room and have Grace work with you?"

Detective Ardley shrugged. "I would prefer you were there. The people seem more comfortable when you're in the room with them."

"I really can't," she said, trying to look as burdened as she felt. "Today we've had another death. And there's a ton of things to be done when that happens. Grace will help you. If there is any problem, she'll call me and I'll come into the room."

"That'll be fine," he said, making it clear he was not happy with it, but he would make do. "That happens a lot here? People dying?"

"We have our share. Mrs. Boyd was the first one to pass away in the past nine months. We don't usually get two in a row. But when you're dealing with elderly, there's no telling."

He nodded as if thinking over what she had said. "There's one more thing. I'd like to examine Mrs. Boyd's rooms and seal them off for a few days."

"Seal them off? What's going on, Detective?" Jessie

asked, her voice pleading for an explanation. "I have a job to do here. And this is going to get in the way."

"Ms. Cummings," he said, "the autopsy on Mrs. Boyd was completed. Though there was nothing conclusive about the cause of death, there were suspicious signs. We'll know more tomorrow when we get the results from the toxicology lab. We are trying to preserve the evidence should this be labeled a crime."

Her shoulders sagged. She felt very tired, suddenly. Damn that bitchy Madeliene. If poor Marjorie Boyd took her own life, this could turn into a mess of trouble. Jacobson must have been talking to Detective Ardley and knew of this development. That was why he was so worried.

"Could we speak privately, Detective?" Jessie asked.

Ardley signaled the two men to wait in the lobby, then closed the door, sat in the chair in front of her desk, and waited.

Jessie Cummings said, "Suicide is not uncommon among the elderly. They face terrible futures either because of some disease, or they become overly depressed. There are hundreds of reasons. Now, I'm afraid that this is what may have happened here. And if it is not handled discreetly the situation could be very ugly."

"Why do you think Mrs. Boyd committed suicide?" he said.

"I don't know if she did or not. I'm only saying it's possible. Please keep that in mind when you do your investigation. Old people have a right to a certain dignity in their death, something we deprive them of as a society. Please treat this gently."

"Did she have any reason to kill herself?"

Jessie Cummings shrugged. "I don't know. They don't confide in me about their problems. I just don't want her memory tarnished for her friends. It is possible her family may know of a reason, or even her doctor.''

He nodded his head, thinking. ''Well, I'll try to be discreet. Now, I'd still like to see her rooms.''

Jessie nodded, and pulled a key from the desk drawer. ''This key will let you in. Room 312. But, I'm afraid, we've already had the apartment cleaned. And Madeliene Allan took Marjorie's things when she was here yesterday, and told us to get rid of anything else.''

He sighed, clearly annoyed.

''People's bowels empty in death, and . . . the smell . . .''

''I understand,'' Ardley said. He took the key, and stood. ''Well, maybe we'll look around, anyway.''

''Grandma's being buried tomorrow,'' Georgie Allan said. ''I thought you ought to know.''

Benny put his arm around the boy's shoulders. He could see the kid was deep inside himself, pushing down the confusion and tears. ''I'll be there, Georgie. She was my friend.'' They were standing by the front desk in the lobby. He guided the boy over to one of the sofas, and they sat down.

''It ain't going to be easy for you, for awhile,'' Benny said. ''But you got to remember that some day you'll see her again. And for now, she's in a better place where there's no suffering, no pain.''

Georgie nodded. Then he appeared ready to speak, hesitated, then said, ''Why do people have to fight so much? You love somebody, why do you fight?''

Benny didn't say anything, he just hugged Georgie tighter with his arm around the boy's shoulders.

''Mom and Dad love each other, don't they?''

Benny made a noncommittal motion with his head.

''I mean, they had to to get married, didn't they?''

''I suppose,'' Benny said.

"Then why are they always fighting?"

Benny shrugged. "I don't know. People have their problems."

"But Grandma's dead. Couldn't they stop fighting for now? Yesterday Dad was hollering really loud at Mom for making them do an autopsy on Grandma. And Mom was hollering right back. He said she wasn't showing respect for Grandma." He hung his head. "Today it was about Grandma's money. Dad said he needed it for the business. Mom said she wasn't going to give him one penny." Then he looked at Benny. "Don't they care about Grandma being dead? I mean, I do. That's what hurts me, Grandma's not being around. Why don't they feel that way?"

"I am sure they do," Peter said. He had seen them on the sofa across the lobby and walked over. "People have various ways of showing or hiding their feelings. Some let the pain come out in other ways. In arguing. In anger. People are not easy to explain."

Benny hugged the boy again. "C'mon, I'll take you home. You don't want them worrying about you on top of everything else."

Georgie shook his head. "It's okay. I got my bicycle." He stood up.

"You sure you'll be all right?" Benny said.

Georgie nodded. There was an aura of sadness around him. "Don't forget Grandma's funeral tomorrow, will you?"

Benny pursed his lips and nodded. "I'll be there."

"I will be there, also," Peter said.

Georgie nodded, then left.

Peter said, "Rather hurried, having the funeral so soon."

"Some people want to get the dead in the ground as soon as possible," Benny said. "Considering the bad blood between Marjorie and her daughter, it's no surprise."

"Benny," Grace said. She had been standing off to the side watching the scene. "The police would like you to come to the card room."

Benny's face screwed up tight. He didn't say anything.

"Please," Grace said. "They're taking everyone's fingerprints . . ."

"I heard," he said, not hiding the anger he felt. "They ain't getting mine without a court order, I'll tell you." He got up and, with a determined step, headed for the card room.

Peter watched him go, and wondered what that was all about.

Blaaat!

"Oh, my!" Betty said, her eyes wide, her hand over her mouth.

Benny broke up laughing. Eleanor had sat down on the chair in the dining room and this awful sound erupted from beneath her. Her face grew red with embarrassment and anger. The others in the dining room were looking over, surprised and smiling. She got up, and Peter came around to the chair. The back of the cushion had been cut open and sewn lightly. He pulled the stitching apart, and pulled out a rubber whoopee cushion that had been slipped into the seat cushion.

"The mad joker strikes again," Peter said. He wanted to laugh as well, but she was so annoyed that he was afraid he'd hurt her feelings more. "I'm sorry," he said.

Eleanor took control of herself, and smiled. "I'm all right. Just took me by surprise." Then she looked at Benny, who was laughing so hard he couldn't contain himself. "Anybody who laughs that hard has to be suspicious." She grinned.

"I agree," Peter said, and smiled. "Where has he been lately? Was he near these chairs?"

Benny was still laughing so hard he could not talk.

Peter held the chair while Eleanor sat down. "If he keeps that up, he will hurt himself." And they all laughed at that.

It was Chris Lassiter who stopped their laughter. He came to the table to take their orders for dinner. But he had the most forlorn look on his face.

Eleanor asked him the question with a look.

"I'm sorry, folks," Chris said, and for the first time, Peter noticed how young the man was. Mid-twenties by best guess. At the start of his life, while Peter was among the ranks of those nearing the end. Peter didn't like what he felt. Chris said, "I heard about Mrs. Templeton. This is hard for me to take. Does this happen often?"

"Only once," Benny said, not covering the sarcasm in his tone. Eleanor gave Benny a look that said he should shut up. Betty delicately rolled her eyes.

Chris ignored the remark. "I've started looking at everyone as if they are going to be next. It's not a pleasant way to work. I mean, I like it here. I like working here. But, now, it's different." He suddenly saw the sad and sympathetic faces looking at him. "I'm sorry. I didn't mean to . . . well, you know what I mean." Then he tried a smile that fell a little short. "Can I take your order for dinner?"

They chose their food without an appetite, except for Benny who ordered as if it were his last meal. Peter thought that, at Benny's age, it just might be. Death was suddenly in everyone's awareness zone. For people their age, death was always hanging around in the background. But now they were forced to look it in the eye. After Chris left, a silence fell over the table, each person inside themselves. Except for Benny, who looked annoyed at their solemnity.

"Can we have this funeral tomorrow?" Benny said.

When no one responded, he said, "I hope you guys aren't going to look this sad when I go. 'Cause it'll make me mad, and then I ain't going to go."

Betty said, in a concerned voice, "Oh, we won't look this sad." There was a moment of realization before everyone giggled at that. Betty suddenly realized how it sounded. "Oh, my. No, I mean we don't want you to be mad. Oh"— she put her hand up in surrender—"you know what I mean."

Benny jumped in to stir things up. "What's Eugene been saying about when I'm going?"

Betty waved her hand at him, to tell him she wasn't going to take him seriously.

"Eugene not speaking to you? He mad at you or something?" Benny ignored the sharp look he got from Eleanor.

As she spoke, Betty's eyes turned toward Peter. "I told him about Peter." She hesitated.

"Oh, Peter." She hesitated.

"Oh, Peter's next? Hell, he just got here."

"Benny," Eleanor said, "put a sock in it."

"No," Betty said, "but he did say that Peter was to be careful. There was a lot of trouble coming his way."

"Okay, Peter." Benny smiled. "It's your turn. Got your will in order?"

Peter gave him a weak grin in response. But Peter felt uneasy. Too uneasy.

CHAPTER
6

The funeral for Marjorie Boyd was mercifully short. Jessie Cummings had gathered together seven people who wanted to attend the funeral, and bused them there in the van. It was a white van with *Coral Sands* in flowing pink on the side. They arrived at the cemetery just before nine-thirty.

There was a quick service at the grave site. Everyone stood in the shade of a large canopy tent that protected them from the sun, but not from the raw heat that cooked the air. A sticky warm front had slipped in overnight and pushed the temperature unusually high for April. In addition to the group from Coral Sands—which included Betty, Eleanor, Peter, and Benny—there were Georgie and his parents, a priest, and two people from the funeral home at the service. Not a large gathering.

Peter stood with the others, the heat sticking his shirt to him. It felt strange to be mourning the dead on such a beautiful day, with nobody wearing black except the priest. Benny didn't help in the serious department; he wore his baseball hat through the entire ceremony. The minister spoke in hallowed tones about the loss of a friend and mother, and the rewards that awaited all of us. Betty wept softly; Eleanor was quiet. Peter drew Benny's attention to a man standing off from the service. It looked like the Cuban he had seen in the lobby that time when Alice, in her clown outfit, had nearly knocked him over. Benny looked hard at the Cuban, then turned back to the ceremony. Jessie also noticed the man. When the minister wound up his speech, Jessie left the group and approached the man.

"Mr. Vasquez," she smiled. "I didn't know you knew Mrs. Boyd. You could have joined us at the grave."

"I did not know the lady," he said in his easy sleepy voice. "I came to see how you respect the death. It is that my mother deserves such respect. I do not want her in a place where this is not done."

"We are family," she said. "One death in the family is important to all of us."

"It is I hear another death," he said.

"Yes," she said, "there are times when we must deal with more than one of the family leaving us." She felt she was sounding like the minister at the grave site.

"It worries me, that there is so much death in your home," he said. There was no expression in his voice, and it unnerved her.

"When there are so many elderly in one place, death sometimes visits us often." Damn, now she sounded more like a funeral director.

"It does not sound natural, your deaths. Perhaps I speak with Mr. Jacobson about this." His mouth moved in a hint of a smile as he turned and walked away.

Now what the hell was that all about? Jessie wondered. She headed for the van.

"Thank you for coming," Richard Allan was saying to Benny and Peter. "It is nice to know she had such friends."

Peter and Benny both nodded without saying anything.

What was there to say? Peter saw that Madeliene, standing next to Richard, was as much angry as sad.

Benny was aware that Georgie was very much inside himself; there was only a cold, distant look on the boy's face. No tears yet. Benny knew they'd come when the time was right. The boy couldn't hold himself so tightly together for long before he'd lose his grip and let out the pain of his loss.

"Georgie," Benny said. "Please come by and visit, will you? I like your company." Then to Richard Allan, "I mean what I just said. Don't discourage him from stopping by. Us old folks need all the company we can get."

"Georgie is free to stop by when he wants," Richard Allan said. Madeliene made a move to speak, but Richard stopped her cold with a look.

"I'll come by and see you, Benny," Georgie said.

"Good," Benny smiled.

The group boarded the van and drove back to Coral Sands. During the ride back, Benny told Peter the poker game had been moved to that night. Peter said he would make it. "Now, don't let us down. We're a little short of players, and we need fresh money." Peter again said he would be there, but that he planned to take money from the game, not contribute. Benny chuckled. "We'll see." When they entered the lobby, Detective Ardley was seated on one of the sofas.

"Ms. Cummings," the detective said and rose heavily, with a grunt of effort. "I would like to speak with you, if I may." Then he saw Peter and Benny as they were about to pass him. "Gentlemen, would you be so kind as to wait." He looked hard at Benny. "Mr. Ashe, if you would wait here a moment. I have a court order I'd like to show you." Then, with a sly grin, Ardley said to Peter, "Ah, but first I would have a word with Mr. Benington."

Peter's heart stopped cold. Though the sweat on his body was from the heat outside, he felt a new heat growing inside him. "Certainly, Detective."

"May I use your office for a few moments?" Ardley said to Jessie.

She hesitated, then nodded.

"After you, Mr. Benington." With a movement of his hand, Ardley indicated the office door.

Peter walked into the office, and waited while Detective Ardley came in behind him and closed the door.

"Please sit down," Ardley said to Peter, as he himself took the chair behind the desk.

Peter sat down. He felt like he was in a box and it was growing tighter around him. His life was catching up to him. He could feel his heart struggling to maintain its rhythm and he began to sweat.

"How well did you know Mrs. Boyd?" Detective Ardley said.

"I made her acquaintance about a month ago when I first came here to sign the papers and make arrangements to move in."

"You went out with her, isn't that so?"

"Yes, we went to dinner that evening, and found we liked each other's company."

"I heard that you stayed the night."

"Yes."

"From what I've also heard, you made a big fuss over her jewelry."

"It is flattering to a woman to admire her taste in jewelry. And she had a necklace of excellent quality."

"Yes, and you are an expert in jewelry and jewel thieves." Ardley leaned forward, his arms on the desk, his hands clasped. His eyes never left Peter's.

"I'm still impressed by the remarkable coincidence that

the day you show up, there is a jewel theft reported. Amazing, isn't it?"

Peter kept his mouth shut. The one thing he had learned in his life was to not volunteer information.

Ardley stared into Peter's eyes and didn't say anything. There was a long moment of silence that Ardley finally broke. "Did she show you the jewelry she had in the safe-deposit box, perhaps?"

"No."

"Did she tell you about it?"

"I don't remember."

"Convenient," Ardley said. "The jewelry that is missing is estimated to be worth about fifty thousand dollars. Did you know that?"

"No. But I'm not surprised, if they were anything of the quality of the necklace she wore."

Ardley watched Peter a long moment before he spoke. "That business of yours must have been very good for you to afford to live here?"

"Yes, it was."

"I am truly amazed that there is that much money to be made in insurance." He shrugged and gave Peter a condescending smile. "I am definitely in the wrong line of work. Maybe someday you could tell me all about your work. It might make a good career change for me." The smile told Peter he didn't believe a word Peter had said about his work.

"I'm going to let you in on a little secret," Ardley said, leaning forward conspiratorially. "We got the report back from toxicology this morning, and Mrs. Boyd was poisoned."

Damn, Peter thought, and his heart started jumping around. He hoped the medication would do its job keeping the beat. The box around him had closed tighter, leaving him barely any breathing room. He struggled to maintain an outward calm, but his throat was tight, and inside it felt like there was an electric current running through him, every muscle thrumming like guitar strings.

"Nothing to say?"

"No."

"You see I'm now having real difficulty with the coincidence. Not only is there a jewel theft the day you arrive, there is also a murder. And the murdered woman was the one with the jewels. You see how this is getting more and more difficult to see as a coincidence?"

Keep control. Breathe easily, Peter kept telling himself, but it wasn't working. He could feel the heat rise in his face. "Are you saying that I had something to do with all this?"

"What I'm saying is that you are my prime suspect, Mr. Benington. And I would not want you to take any trips for awhile. I'd hate to have to put you on a wanted list. You do understand?"

Peter nodded. He felt suddenly old and tired.

"That's all I have for you, right now, Mr. Benington. But I'm sure we'll be talking again."

Peter rose, his legs shaking, and turned toward the door.

"Oh, yes," Ardley said. "There is one more thing that really tests all this coincidence. I have a witness that says you were the last person to see Mrs. Boyd alive. In fact you went into her apartment with her." He let that hang in the air.

Peter stood frozen, it had to be that drunken woman they'd seen in the hall. Breathing was getting impossible, his throat tight like a hand was choking him, and he could feel the sweat forming on his face and running down his back beneath the shirt.

"So *many* coincidences, don't you think?" Ardley said, stressing the word "many."

Peter remained standing and said nothing. His mind was locked up with fear and a desperate weariness.

"You didn't perhaps mix her a little drink of arsenic and strychnine while you were in the apartment with her, did you?" Ardley grinned. It was a grin that said, I got you bad.

Peter turned and put his hand on the doorknob. He wanted to get out of there quickly. Ardley said to Peter's back, "I would find myself a good lawyer, if I were you, Mr. Benington."

Peter opened the door and stepped out. The air seemed cooler outside the office. He took some deep breaths that were difficult to get past the knot in his throat. Benny was sitting nearby on a sofa, and he didn't look like a happy camper. They exchanged glances, but said nothing. Peter walked across the lobby. He wanted to run, to run away. Hell, he thought he had run away—to this place. This was to be the serene park where he could sit back on a bench, look at the sky, and let the years quietly drain the life from him. The park had turned into a carnival fun house, and it was scaring him to death.

Betty saw him and waved her excited little wave. She was sitting in the coffee alcove with Eleanor. Peter's first thought was to wonder what else Eugene had to say.

Grace came off the elevator and, without acknowledging him, walked past Peter toward the office. She was a woman on a mission; her face locked in hard stone, her mind focused elsewhere. Peter was glad he didn't have to smile a greeting. Smiling was the last thing he felt like doing.

Betty was still waving at him, obviously wanting him to join them. Peter gave a small wave back to her, but couldn't manage a smile. He got on the elevator, went up to the third floor, and headed toward his apartment. He passed Mr. Petersen who was dancing sprightly down the hall, moving about with his arms up like he had a dancing partner. Petersen was humming a tune as he danced. As Peter passed by the man, he said, "We do not need Fred Astaire right now, Mr. Petersen. We need Sherlock Holmes."

"Corrine Medford?" Jessie Cummings asked, and she glanced at Detective Ardley. *Damn.*

Grace nodded, her face clouded with concern.

Detective Ardley had been telling Jessie Cummings about Marjorie Boyd being poisoned, when Grace came into the office with the news that a third person had died. As Grace explained about this latest death, Detective Ardley's expression grew unreadable, and his whole body relaxed as if under a heavy weight. "Before you discuss this further," he said, his voice even and cold, "I must advise you that, in light of Marjorie's poisoning, I consider this death and the one yesterday as suspicious. And I want the area and the body to remain untouched until we have examined them. I want an autopsy performed on each of the bodies. I'll get the necessary court order." Then to Jessie Cummings, "I would like to use your phone." He picked up the telephone without waiting for her reply.

Jessie said to Grace, "Please get Jacobson on the phone for me." *This should really make his day,* she thought.

As Ardley punched in the numbers, he said, "And Grace, would you ask Mr. Ashe to come in here. I need to get his fingerprints."

"Mom and Dad are having just terrible fights," Georgie Allan was saying to Betty. He really wanted to talk to Benny. Benny would understand. But he wasn't around. And Georgie couldn't hold his hurt inside any longer. It was building like steam in a boiler and needed a release. So, he let some of it out to Betty. She was a nice old lady, and wouldn't get angry with him.

"Oh, well," Betty said. She was sitting next to Georgie on a sofa, trying to console the boy. "As Eugene, my husband, used to say, marriages have their bumpy times. Now, don't you worry so much about it. Benny will tell you the same thing when he gets out of the office with that policeman."

"Mom said last night she was going to get a divorce." Georgie was trying his best to keep the real hurt inside.

"Oh, pooh," Betty said, waving away Georgie's concern. "When they are angry, people say such things to get attention. They don't mean them."

Georgie did not believe her. "It really sounded like she meant it. And Dad told her to go ahead. But he'd take his share of everything, if she did. It was awful."

Betty didn't say anything. She just put her plump little hand on Georgie's knee, and gently patted it.

Georgie's face suddenly screwed up with emotion, the hurt now fighting to get out. "Don't they care that Grandma died? All they do is fight about Grandma's money."

Betty patted his knee some more. "I'm sure they miss her very much. But it's hard to talk about such things, sometimes."

"They never once said they cared." Tears welled in the boy's eyes. "Grandma was a good person." He stopped and fought back the tears. "They didn't love her. Why? She was so nice." Then Georgie clamped down on the torrent that wanted to burst from him. It was a torrent of confusion and anger and pain. He sniffled, wiped at the tears, and pushed the emotion back inside.

"It will be all right," Betty said, her hand still gently patting his knee.

He held himself tight, and prepared to say what he had come for. "You think Benny could talk to them?" The hope was there in every word. He saw Betty's expression change and knew she didn't think so. "I mean, they would listen to him," he said, trying to convince her that it might be a good idea. "Adults don't listen to children. But they do listen to other adults."

"Well," she sighed. She saw how hurt and desperate the boy was. "We could ask him. Maybe Benny could think of something."

It was at that moment Benny, scowling, came out of the office, wiping his fingers with a paper towel.

"What the hell is going on over there!" Jacobson was shouting into the phone. Jessie held the receiver away from her ear. "You trying to ruin me? I got a telephone call from a reporter this morning. Says he wanted to know what I had to say about the murders at Coral Sands. *Murders!* He's already counting the death yesterday as a second murder. And now you're telling me there's another one! This gets in the newspapers and—God forbid—on television, that there's a murderer on the loose in the Home and the place'll empty out."

Jessie jumped in when he took a breath. "The police have not determined that there was a murder, yet."

"Yet!" he screamed. "That's the key word! The newspapers aren't going to wait for that confirmation! When they get wind of this third death, that's all they'll need! What the hell are the police doing about this anyway? They checking the staff? Anyone we hired recently?"

"The police've been underfoot here, if that's what you mean," she said. "But you'll have to talk to them about what they're doing. All I can tell you is their being here is starting the rumors flying.''

"Talk to them!" Jacobson said. "Talk is all it is. Is Ardley still working on this?''

"Yes," she said. "He's upstairs right now with other policemen, checking out Corrine Medford's apartment.''

"Jesus," he said. "All I've worked for.'' This time he was talking to himself aloud.

"Is this going to affect the sale price of the Home?'' Jessie had to say it. She had suspected, now she had to know.

There was silence on the other end. Then Jacobson spoke softly. "Who have you been talking to?''

"I keep my ear to the ground," she said.

"Who told you this?''

In for a penny, in for a pound. "One of the potential customers mentioned it.''

"Who?''

"A Mr. Vasquez," she said. "Do you know him?''

"He was there! Jesus." His voice remained soft and low. No shouting now. There was a long moment of silence, then he hung up.

Jessie looked at the telephone, put the receiver back in its cradle, and her heart felt flat. She liked her job, liked the people. She didn't classify them as old people, but as people who were old. And they were her friends. She helped them, made their world comfortable and pleasant, and she watched them grow very old and die. In her heart each death had its own pain, but she accepted it, and turned to comforting her friends who were still living.

She had believed this job, this lifestyle would go on as long as she wanted. Jacobson would always be there grouching a little; Grace ever joking and laughing; and even

Benny, who seemed determined to know every resident and help them get acclimated and involved in the community of the Home. There was a comfortable feeling in all that. Now, she saw, even here things never stayed the same.

Jessie's world was going to change, and she was afraid.

CHAPTER
7

Peter planned to spend the rest of the day in his apartment trying to get a hold on the situation he found himself in; trying to assess the box that was closing in on him, and figure a way out. There were always alternatives, he kept telling himself. But running away and leaving everything behind was the only one he had come up with so far.

When Peter was younger leaving was an alternative that would have had merit. Back then he could always earn a living and rebuild his possessions. Now, however, he had neither the energy nor the opportunities. He was a member of the unemployable—the senior citizen. Or as Benny would say—the senile citizen. Peter could find work, but it would be sweeping the floors at the local convenience store for less than the minimum wage. That was, if the arthritis in his hip didn't give him too much trouble. And if his heart arrhythmia didn't act up. Jesus.

He had indulged himself with two glasses of Amaretto even though it was barely noon. He thought of what Eleanor had said about how some things were better faced with a little alcohol. And he thought that maybe a lot of alcohol would be even better. Maybe he would get stinking drunk and lose himself in the dark haze of booze. He hadn't done that in a long time. It wouldn't solve any problems, but for the short term it would feel good. The temptation to do just that grew stronger with the second Amaretto. And he probably would have followed through with his plan if Benny hadn't knocked on his door. The skinny old man in the baseball cap. He wondered if Benny ever took the cap off.

"I see you're celebrating early," Benny said, smirking at the drink in Peter's hand.

Peter said nothing, but instead raised his glass lightly as if in a toast.

"I need your help," Benny continued, his gaze meeting Peter's steadily, as if reading everything Peter was thinking. "I'll come right to the point. No beating around the bush. Georgie was here today and he got Betty all worked up about the trouble at home. He wants me to speak with his old man. 'Cause adults don't listen to kids, he said. And he's right. Though, adults don't listen to adults either, if you don't say things they want to hear. You following?"

Peter nodded. "I understand the words, if that's what you are referring to."

"Close enough. Eleanor was saying that it's none of my business and I should keep my nose out of it. Kids grow up and all this stuff is so much forgotten bullshit." Benny shrugged. "At least that's the gist of what she said. Betty was giving me that screwed up, hurting look and telling me to do something for the kid. And Georgie just looked at me with pleading eyes. Finally I said if I stick my nose in, then it's my business, too. Something like that."

"So, you're going to speak with Richard Allan. Is that what you are saying to me?" Peter asked, and absently took a sip of his drink while waiting for Benny to get to the point.

"Yeah. I figure it can't hurt. If the asshole doesn't like what he hears, he throws me out. No big deal. I got no relationship with him to worry me. And I'm an old man. What do I care what he thinks about me." Then he stopped.

Peter waited for more. When nothing came, he said, "And what sort of help are you expecting from me?"

"Thanks, I knew you'd do it," Benny said with relief.

"Do what?"

"Come with me and speak with Dick Allan."

"Wait one minute . . ."

"Look, I talk to the guy, I'm only gonna piss him off. I'm not too good with words unless I'm threatening somebody, or being a smartass. But you, you're slick. You got that charm that makes people listen to you. They listen to the words you're saying and don't react to the look on your face. Me, as soon as people see my face, how angry I am, they don't hear the words at all. You know what I mean?"

"I'm not sure about this."

"Look, what do you care? You don't even know the guy. You say your piece, and we'll keep each other company when they throw us out. But at least we can say we tried. And, who knows, maybe the guy'll listen and we help the kid. Problem?"

Problem? Hell, suddenly all he had were problems.

Richard Allan took them right into his office which was just inside the entrance to the building, a large blue and white metal-skinned box with a couple of truck bays and a single door. There was a sign in blue script—BOAT DECOR. Peter was impressed by the man's office, considering what was just outside the door. Done in wood paneling, it was decorated with old maps, pictures of sailing ships, and all sorts of sailing brass: compasses, barometers, clocks, sextants, and fittings. To Peter, some of them looked like antiques. Richard Allan smiled and gestured them to sit down. Peter and Benny each took one of the two comfortable chairs facing the broad, wood desk.

"I know the decor is a little hokey," Richard Allan said, as he sat in the chair behind the desk. "But it's a nice way to display our products. Here they have that real nautical look—old time sailing ships and Captain Ahab—that sailors like to picture themselves being a part of. The brass has a naked look when seen on the warehouse floor. So this is where the customers first see them."

"If they get past the pile of muscle at the secretary's desk outside," Benny said. It had bothered him to be confronted by a tough, muscled guy sitting where a pretty secretary should have been. "I'd think he'd scare them away."

Peter noticed that at first Richard Allan saw no humor in the remark, but he quickly recovered, and gave Benny a winning smile. "On the contrary, Herman's there to see they don't change their minds once they get this far. I suspect he may even intimidate them to not leave empty-handed."

"You deal with individual customers?" Peter said.

"Really only to a small degree. I used to work for Wellcraft, so when I bought this business seven years ago, I negotiated a nice contract with them. And we put out a catalogue that the boat brokers show their customers. Like I said, with the antique designs of our products we give the boater a feeling of being in touch with the dramatic sailing ships of old. You know, the sailing adventures on the high seas." Then he leaned back in the chair. "Now what can I do for you, gentlemen?"

Benny looked to Peter.

"I will not take up time—as Americans say—beating

about the bush." Peter kept his voice low, and sat with relaxed confidence. "We're here about your son, Georgie." The smile left Richard Allan's face, and he focused hard on Peter. "No," Peter said. "Nothing has happened to the boy, and he hasn't done anything to be ashamed of. Let me ease your mind about that." Richard Allan's expression did not change. He was still looking hard at Peter, waiting for the shoe to drop. "From the few times I have met him, I can say that he is a boy any man would be proud to have as a son."

Benny said to Peter, "I thought you weren't going to beat around the bush."

Peter gave them both a warm, friendly smile. "Yes, I apologize. We are here on Georgie's behalf. The death of his grandmother has been a shock to him. He needs comforting, reassuring, understanding. He has said, quite frankly, that you and your wife have been spending your time arguing over his grandmother's money, and no time mourning her death." Richard Allan's face showed anger flashing about under the surface.

"Please, we are not here to accuse you of anything." Peter was concerned the man would jump up and start shouting. "We are sure that you have not treated his grandmother's death flippantly. We simply want you to know the boy's view. Whatever you may be experiencing, he does not see you mourning his loss. He has expressed his concern to us because, it appears, he has no one else to talk to. We thought you should be aware of this. Sometimes during the emotional upheaval such tragedies bring on a family, the grief is not shared with the children. Their pain and loss is not attended to." All the while Peter spoke, he watched the anger fade from Richard Allan's face. In its place was an expression of concern. "We sincerely hope you will forgive us for intruding like this. We felt that possibly you weren't aware of Georgie's hurt. And there was a chance that once you knew, you could help him.'' Peter stopped and waited.

Benny looked at Peter with admiration. The man certainly could slick his way around, he thought.

After a moment Richard Allan brought a hand to his forehead and pulled the hand down over his face, wiping away the fatigue that had suddenly found its way there. ''I'm sorry you had to get involved in this,'' Richard Allan said, a weariness in his voice. ''It's been a tough time for us. The business has been good lately, but not good enough to dig out from under the debt we were forced to take on a few years back when the Feds slapped that luxury tax on the boating industry. The tax lasted only a couple of years, but during that time, the boating industry fled the country.'' He waved his hand around the room. ''And there was no market for all this. None. They were desperate times. To keep the business afloat, I borrowed until there were no more people willing to lend me money.'' His shoulders sagged with the weight he was carrying. ''I may have shown concern over Marjorie's money, because with it I can get the business out of this debt. You know her estate was over seven hundred thousand dollars. With that the business could get back to normal. But Maddie, Madeliene is afraid to let go of the money. And, well . . .'' He stopped, realization suddenly in his eyes. He smiled weakly. ''I'm sorry. I guess I don't have someone to talk to, either. I appreciate your concern for my son. I love him very much. With my own problems, I guess I didn't see how much he was hurting over Marjorie's death. I promise you I'll try to make it up to him. I want to thank you for coming to me with this. Believe me, Marjorie's death has been hard on all of us.''

Peter recognized that an awkward point had been

reached. He stood. "You need not explain, Mr. Allan. But we do understand. Thank you for your time. And we wish you well."

Benny stood with reluctance. He wanted to hear what else Richard Allan had to say.

They left the office. In the reception area just outside the office, Benny turned to Herman who was still seated at the secretary's desk, the man's muscles pushed tightly against the polo shirt he wore. "You ever have to sit in the boss's lap?"

Peter grabbed Benny's arm as Herman stood up to his full height and looked down at Benny with a threatening expression. Herman stood six two, if an inch, and had more muscle than a gang of stevedores.

"Come on, Benny," Peter said as, still holding him by the arm, he drew Benny away. Outside in the parking lot the air was heavy with heat. Peter said, "Benny, your mouth is going to get you a great many broken bones one day."

"Naw. People don't get all riled up over some old man who's probably crazy." Benny, eyes narrowed, looked back over his shoulder at the building. "Besides, I think I could still take that creep."

Peter snorted, but didn't reply. He couldn't get over the arrogance of this little old man. Skinny and short, with that silly baseball cap on his head, tipping the time scale in the seventies, and still talking like some tough hoodlum.

Betty and Eleanor were in Benny's Mercury Marquis, vintage 1978, waiting for them to come out. The women had insisted on coming with Peter and Benny when they found out the men were going to talk to Richard Allan. In fact, they had also wanted to come inside, but Benny had put his foot down. Peter had also insisted the ladies stay outside. They didn't want to have Richard Allan feel they were ganging up on him. Betty treated this whole experience with the excitement of a child on an outing for the first time.

When Peter and Benny got back in the front of the car, Eleanor asked, "Well, how did the mercy mission go?"

Benny shrugged. "He listened, and didn't throw us out. That's a good sign. And you should have heard the ambassador here." Indicating Peter with a nod of his head. "Talk about smooth. This guy was great."

Peter gave them an it-was-nothing shrug.

"You think he'll talk to Georgie?" Betty said.

"His reaction was positive, and sincere," Peter said. "He did confide in us the money problems he has with the business, and that Marjorie's money would bail him out of much of that. But his wife won't agree to putting her inheritance into the business. The gentlemen has problems."

Eleanor said, "I don't want to spend the rest of the day sitting here in this parking lot. How about you take us out of here, Benny?"

"Maybe take us to that restaurant on the beach?" Betty said.

"Can't. Got a date for dinner." Benny said, then started the car and backed out of the parking space. "And Peter and I have the poker game at seven o'clock tonight." Peter raised an eyebrow in question. "So, I forgot to tell you. You going to come or not? My place."

Peter nodded. "Yes. Why not. If you're going to be there this time."

Benny ignored him.

"She must be some hot number, Benny," Eleanor taunted. "When are we going to meet her?"

"Yes," Betty said. "Why don't you bring her around so we can see this creature who's taken your heart?" She said it with a giggle behind all the words.

"I don't want her to think bad of me, by the company I keep," Benny said, and drove the car out of the parking lot, barely missing a long, white Cadillac with dark windows that was pulling into the lot. Benny had to pull off to the side to keep from hitting the car. "Jesus!" Benny said, looking back at the car pulling up to the door. "Why don't people learn to drive those things?" He was about to turn back to the front when a man Benny recognized got out of the back of the cadillac. "Hey, ain't that the Cuban guy from Marjorie's funeral?"

Peter turned around. So did the two women.

"It appears to be the same man," Peter said, wondering at how small this town was that they kept running into this same guy. First at the Home, then Marjorie's funeral, and now going in to see Richard Allan.

"I didn't see him at the funeral," Betty said.

"Neither did I," Eleanor said.

"He was standing back a ways. Not with us," Benny said. "I wonder what he's doing with Georgie's father?"

"Probably owns a boat," Peter said.

"Yeah," Benny said, with no conviction. He was beginning to worry. "Wonder what he was doing at the funeral?"

"Jessie walked over and spoke to him," Peter said. He picked up on Benny's concern, and wondered why Benny was troubled.

"Yeah," Benny said. His voice was low and distant, as if he were speaking aloud to himself. "And he was in the Home the other morning. Sure gets around, that guy. Wonder who he is?"

"This is so exciting!" Betty gushed. "A real mystery!" she said, also picking up on Benny's concern. "Can I be Miss Jane Marple? I love those mysteries. She's so smart."

Eleanor, too, picked up on Benny's concern, but she didn't say anything. She just sat there thinking about it.

Peter begged off from dinner with Eleanor and Betty. He still had to think his way out of the mess that was rapidly building around him. But the solitude of the apartment didn't bring him any new ideas. Just a desperate feeling. He felt old and trapped. He made himself a bite to eat in his apartment, but the food had no taste. Then at seven he went down to Benny's apartment to join the poker game. He had thought of begging off the poker game, too, but couldn't come up with a good excuse.

Benny's apartment was 208, directly beneath Peter's, and was exactly the same layout. But the furniture and decor of Benny's apartment could only be classified as early Salvation Army. Clean, but an array of discarded fashions.

When Peter arrived, they were already seated at the table—one that looked like the metal-top kitchen table his mother threw out when he was just a boy. Everybody nodded to him as he took the empty chair. Peter was introduced to Walter Innes, a doctor of medicine retired. Innes was a gaunt man with knobby and sagging features, long bony hands, and short gray hair in disarray. A wood cane was hooked on the back of his chair. Next Peter met Charlie Aspen, a big man whose large belly pushed hard at the buttons of the shirt he wore. Charlie had retired early from some corporation where he headed up the Berlin office. Besides Benny, the only other player was Alice Chomseky.

"Hiya, handsome," she said with a suggestive smile. "Maybe we should change the game to strip poker."

Benny said, with disgust, "C'mon, Alice, I just ate."

Charlie Aspen chuckled. "At our age, with all the wrinkles, it would look like ironing day at the laundry."

Everyone laughed.

"Deal, Alice," Benny said. "Anyone want a beer or anything?"

The beer order went around, and Benny retrieved the cans from the refrigerator. Peter opened his can, and took a large gulp. The cold beer tearing at his throat tasted good.

The first few hands showed Peter that these people took their poker very seriously, even in a nickel-dime game. The luck of the cards was coming his way, but he didn't gain as much from the hands as he should have because they played so tight to the chest. There was no steady talking through the game. Conversation came in bits and spurts.

"How's your knee?" Walter Innes said to Alice.

"No problem," Alice shrugged. "Except I get a pain now and then." She took two dimes and tossed them into the pot. "I raise a dime."

Charlie and Benny called her bet.

"You were lucky not to have damaged the knee more than you did. Somersaults are not recommended at your age," Walter said. "I call," he said, and put his money in the middle of the table.

"Hey, it got the kids' attention."

"So did the arrival of the ambulance, I'm sure."

"Was the highlight of the party," Alice grinned. "They want me back, but only if I bring the ambulance again."

"You're not using the walker anymore?" Charlie said.

"I still got it in the trunk of my car, just in case."

Peter jumped at what sounded like an explosion outside. Then rain slammed against the windows of the apartment.

"Relax, handsome," Alice said, not looking up from her cards. "It's only a Florida storm. You in?"

Benny said, "Save your jumping for the summer—when we get a good soaker with the whole light and sound show for about a half hour almost every afternoon."

Peter threw in twenty cents. "I call."

"And twenty minutes later it looks like it never rained." Alice laid her cards on the table. "Two pair, aces up."

The others threw their cards down. Peter looked with disappointment at the pair of kings and fours in his hand, then folded his hand.

"Didn't see you at the mourners' lunch today," Alice said to Peter, as she pulled the money toward her.

Peter shrugged his shoulders. "I didn't really know the woman." It was a lame response, but no one pursued it. "I bet a dime."

"Elaine Singleton was there," Alice said. She shuffled the cards and dealt them out. "God, she's looking awful. Nothing left on her but skin and bones."

"Won't have to embalm her," Benny said. "She'll be preserved for the next two centuries with all that booze in her."

"They'll have to be careful lighting candles at her funeral," Charlie said.

Benny looked at his cards, then put five cents in the pot. "I open for a nickel."

"Saw Ted Walden and his wife there," Walter Innes said, his long hands trembling as he held his cards. "She's going down fast." He threw in his dime. "Call."

Peter called.

"It's awful, Alzheimer's. Eats away your brain," Alice said. "Don't know who you are anymore. Don't know who anyone is. Can't even dress yourself." Alice shook her head sadly. "Sure makes you wonder where the idea of a merciful God came from." She took a moment more to examine her cards. "Raise a dime," she said and threw in twenty cents.

Charlie Aspen shook his head sadly. "I watched my father die of the damn disease. Wasn't something I'd want to do again."

Walter Innes said, "There's a hereditary factor associated with the disease. You're more likely to get it if one of
your parents had it."

"Thanks, Doc, for the news report," Charlie said, annoyed, and threw his cards in. "I know all about that, and
it scares the shit out of me. I get nightmares sometimes that
I got it. So, please could we talk about something else."

"First signs are you forget how to do simple things,"
Alice said.

"Like pick your nose," Benny said, with his smart
mouth. "Are we playing poker or taking a course in medical school?" He called the bet.

"No, like forgetting how to do arithmetic. Or turn on
the windshield wipers. Stuff like that," Alice said, then she
looked around the table. "I raised. Who's still in?"

"I'll never know I got it then," Benny said, "because I
stink at arithmetic. And I haven't ever been able to figure
out the windshield wipers on my car."

"Call," Walter Innes and Peter said. And Alice meekly
showed her full house. Everyone groaned.

"Any news on the theft of the silverware?" Charlie said,
as he started gathering the cards together, trying to get off
the subject of Alzheimer's. It made him sick to think about
the disease. He'd have cold sweats in the night, thinking
how his father had suffered and died, and how he might be
next.

"Other than Manuel's gonna have a baby over it," Alice
Chomseky said, stacking the coins she pulled in from the
pot.

"Yeah," Benny said. "Manuel thinks someone's opening a restaurant with our silverware and dishes. He should
be concerned he's got a job after the Home is sold."

Everyone looked at Benny. "Where'd you hear that?"
Charlie said.

"I got my sources," Benny said. "Seems Jacobson has the place for sale, is what I heard. That's all I know. C'mon and deal, Charlie."

There was a hesitation as everyone mulled over this news, trying to figure how things would change if it were true.

"I hear the police think those three women were poisoned," Charlie said, trying to keep them talking so they won't go back to Alzheimer's. He picked up the cards and started shuffling them.

"Murdered," Alice Chomseky said, with emphasis.

Benny made a sound with his mouth that said it was nonsense.

"Benny," Charlie Aspen said. He stopped shuffling the cards and put them on the table. "How about another deck? These cards don't like me. Maybe it'll change my luck."

"Sure." Benny reached to the counter behind him, took another box of cards, and tossed them across the table to Charlie. Charlie handed him the old deck.

"Murder is a strong word when you are dealing with the elderly," Walter Innes said. "In my years of practice I've seen many who have taken their own lives rather than go on suffering the loneliness and despair to reach the certain death that awaits us all."

"Five card draw, jacks or better," Charlie said, and started dealing out the cards. "Everyone ante?"

They all put ten cents in the pot. The cards slipped easily from Charlie's hand, landing carefully in front of each of them.

"It could still be murder," Alice Chomseky said.

"Who would want to murder these three women?" Peter said.

"Their husbands," Benny said with a smirk.

"They were all widows," Alice said.

"Hell, more than half the joint is widows. Work the old man to death, then live on his life savings and insurance."

"Maybe only one of them is the real victim?" Alice Chomseky said. "You know, kill the others to hide who the real victim is?"

"You reading too many mysteries again, Alice."

"What about the jewelry, there's a motive?" Alice wasn't going to give up.

"That's petty theft, not a motive for murdering anybody."

"Well, the police are going to fingerprint everybody in the place to find out who stole the jewelry. I think they'll find the killer, too."

Charlie Aspen stopped dealing, and frowned at Alice. "Where did you hear that? They're going to fingerprint everybody?"

"You worried they'll find out you did it?" Benny smirked. "C'mon, deal."

Peter noticed that not only did Charlie Aspen suddenly look worried, but there was also a serious expression on the face of Walter Innes. Maybe they had the same things to worry them as he did—dark skeletons in the past.

Charlie dealt out the last few cards more slowly, thinking about the fingerprinting.

"What the . . . !" Alice had picked up her cards and was looking at them in surprise. Then she started laughing in a loud bellow. "Goddamn!"

The others were looking wide-eyed at their cards. And Benny started laughing uncontrollably. Peter picked up his cards and saw the queen of hearts was naked and had the biggest pair of breasts a woman could be burdened with. He smiled and looked to Benny who was doubled over laughing, with tears forming in his eyes.

"I believe these cards could be quite distracting to the poker game," Walter Innes said dryly.

"I think I could win with this hand," Charlie Aspen said. "But if I lost, I wouldn't mind much."

"The position of these two people is one I've never seen before," Walter Innes said, using his clinical tone. "Very instructive."

"Some of these bring back fond memories," Alice Chomseky giggled.

CHAPTER

8

The poker game broke up at eleven. Peter was out five plus dollars. So much for his skill at the cards. Alice Chomseky was the clear winner with $22.60 of everyone's money. Benny caught Peter's arm and asked him to stay as the others were leaving the apartment.

"Are you sure you won't admit to putting that deck of cards in play?" Peter said with a grin.

Benny smiled. "I wish it had been my idea. I thought it was terrific. But, I got to admit the mad joker sure has a sense of humor."

"You said to me that the mad joker breaks up the monotony around here. To be truthful, I've been here but a few days, and it has not been monotonous at all. Far from it."

"Yeah," Benny said, "you seem to have brought a lot of excitement with you."

"Me?" Peter's eyebrow arched.

"Look, Slick," Benny said, suddenly very serious, "I got to talk to you about something. Why don't you sit down? I'll get you a drink. A little nightcap. I got some

Scotch in the cabinet. Good stuff. Save it for special company.''

"Is this going to take long? I am very tired, and I would really like to turn in. It has been much too exciting a day, for me."

"How about that Scotch? On the rocks, maybe?"

Peter saw the man needed to talk, and there was no getting away from him. "All right. But straight up. No ice."

"Good. Take a seat," Benny said, sounding relieved. He pointed to the sofa. While Peter made himself comfortable on the sofa, Benny went into the kitchen area, took the bottle of Scotch from the kitchen cabinet, and poured an inch into a rocks glass. He brought the glass to Peter, and took a seat in the stuffed chair next to the sofa. Benny leaned back in the chair and looked at Peter.

"I got to admit you're pretty good, Slick. I'm hoping you're as good as I think you are." He hesitated a moment, trying to find a way in. "Don't you think it's really odd that Cuban guy shows his face here the day Marjorie died? And then he's at her funeral, and then we see him go in to see Marjorie's son-in-law? Real coincidence. And I get nervous about coincidences."

"You and Detective Ardley." Peter took a sip of his Scotch.

"I need your help, Slick. I got to find out more about this guy."

Peter frowned a question he didn't ask.

"All I could get outta Grace was his name—Vasquez." Benny raised his hand to stop Peter's next question. "Grace and I had a little thing going many years back. She keeps me up on what's going on. I get the scoop on every resident from her. That's how I know all about everybody. But here, with this guy, all she could give me was his name. She got that because he called to make an appointment with Jessie.

I need you to talk to Jessie and get whatever she's got on him."

"I'm sorry, Benny," Peter said. "But I don't see how I can do that."

"What's to do? You give her some of that slick talk of yours and she opens up. No big deal."

"Why don't you speak with her?"

" 'Cause she won't tell me anything. I don't have that smooth gift with the tongue that you have."

"Benny, why should I help you do something like this? I don't even know why you want to find out about this man."

"It's really important to me, Slick. You gotta help me with this."

"Benny, you're bringing me into the middle of something that is none of my business. I have enough problems of my own without this. Why did you think I would help you?"

"Because I know you took Marjorie's jewelry." Benny was frowning hard at Peter, communicating with only his facial expression.

Peter sat, silently sipping his Scotch and looking at Benny, wondering what the man was up to. He had to move cautiously, and not get on the Benny's bad side. This skinny, old man in the baseball cap could make real trouble. Peter no longer hoped that somehow all this trouble would work itself out. He now had to deal with this head-on.

"Suppose you tell me what this is all about?" Peter asked.

"Let's just keep that my secret," Benny said.

"If you need me as badly as you say, then I have a bargaining chip in this negotiation. You tell me what's going on, or I don't cooperate."

"That cop Ardley doesn't scare you, huh?" Benny said.

Peter looked patiently at Benny.

After a few moments of silence, Benny sighed and re-laxed. "All right. I do need you. I got no one else to help me. You see, I made a mistake. I was stupid, and now I got to find a way to stop things before they get worse." Benny took a reluctant deep breath. "I got to trust you. Never been that stupid before, to have to trust somebody—except my wife. But I don't see what else I can do. I like it here, and I'm too old to get up and move. You know what I mean? So, I'm stuck with you."

Peter sipped the Scotch and said nothing.

"I think there's a guy out there who's gonna try and kill me."

Whoa, Peter thought. *Benny's another crazy?*

"I know how that sounds. Especially in a place like this, filled with some pretty weird old people. But you gotta listen to me. Hear me out and then make your own decision on what kinda nut I am.

"First, that Cuban is a bad guy. If he was Italian, I'd say he was connected. And don't look at me like that. I know bad guys. I can pick up on a crook. Sort of like, if you hang around them, pretty soon you smell the difference, the things that make them. You meet them in a crowd, and you can pick them out.

"Second, my real name ain't Benny Ashe. It's Mario Socorro. My street name was Socks. That is, all the guys called me Socks. I had a pizza business in Manhattan, down in Little Italy. My wife and I made the best pizza in the world. No lie. We had a good business. But we also had another business. You heard of policy? Numbers?"

Peter nodded, still holding the Scotch.

"Well, I took a lot of bets for Bobby Dee. The guy's last name was DiMarco. Anyway, we took the bets, and once a day just before we closed, a guy would come by and pick up the slips and the money. Naturally, I never gave him all the receipts and money. I always took a couple for me. We did so good at the policy business, they never caught on. It meant to me and Angela about a hundred a week. Not much. But we did this for a lot of years. And we put that away for us. We didn't have any kids. I cursed God over that when I was younger. But looking back, I'm glad we didn't. The trouble and the neighborhood, it wasn't a good place to bring up a kid." He shrugged. "I'm a good example of that." He had been looking away while he spoke, as if seeing it all on the wall opposite his chair. Now he looked at Peter. "I'm not telling this too good."

He settled himself in the chair so he was looking directly at Peter. "Let me get to the point. I'm in the Witness Protection Program. Been in it close to sixteen years. You see, I testified against Bobby Dee and he got sent up for twenty-five to life. Out on good behavior in twenty. Anyway, Bobby Dee and his friends don't take kindly to people testifying against them. Bobby Dee said in the courtroom that I wouldn't be able to hide from him, no matter what. I done pretty good about him not finding me. But I tell you, I been looking over my shoulder every day for the past fourteen years. You see the first two years, I didn't worry. Hell, the Feds were really protecting my ass. Then I almost walked into a bullet sent by Bobby Dee. How he found me, I don't know. But the Feds picked me up again and gave me another name and stuff, and I ended up here. Since then I've been looking over my shoulder like a scared rabbit. I know everybody that moves into this place. I size them up and make sure I'm not dealing with another gun guy or friend of Bobby Dee."

"I saw the way you looked at that Cuban," Peter said. "You think he is after you?"

"I'm not too sure about that. But he is in a position that

might be bad for me when they come back with my fingerprints.''

"Benny, I don't understand . . . never mind. You tell it
your way,'' Peter said.

"You see, the Feds do a great job. Well, maybe not so
great sometimes. But I'm afraid when that cop Ardley gets
my prints back from Washington, somebody may come
with them.''

Washington! Peter thought. *Damn.* If he's sending
Benny's prints to Washington, then he must be sending
Peter's as well.

"Ardley tell you he's sending your fingerprints to Washington?''

"Yeah. He said I smelled funny, and he was going to
check me out. Especially after I made him get a court order.
That was the stupid part. If I had just let him take my prints,
they might not have gone anywhere. But I got scared and
needed time to think. I figured the court order would give
me that time. It did, too, but I didn't think of anything to
do.''

The situation keeps getting worse, Peter thought. *Ardley
will have more information to use against me.*

"You see, the only way Bobby Dee and his guys can
find me is if they're watching when my fingerprints are
looked at. Somebody, some clerk sees my name come
across her desk, tips them, and I've been found.''

"I'm not sure how that can happen,'' Peter said. "Won't
your fingerprints be filed with your new name?''

"Yeah,'' Benny sighed. "But somehow the old stuff is
never gone. And there have been screwups. I said I didn't
know how Bobby Dee found me last time. That's not true.
The guy sent to do me said I shouldn't apply for a job that
requires checking me out with the FBI. That's all I know.
He didn't say no more. You see, the Feds got me a job as

a security guard, and I had to be bonded. How did I know they were going to check with the FBI?''

''Did the Federal Officers question him further to discover how he found you?''

Benny shook his head. ''They don't have the right techniques to talk to the dead.''

Peter looked at the seemingly harmless old man and couldn't fit Benny into the story he'd been telling. Killing a guy? Didn't seem possible.

''You appear to have paid a high price for testifying.''

''I couldn't walk away from that one. With the guys I knew, you didn't talk about that stuff. You turned away. But that one was different.'' Benny took a deep breath and let out a noisy sigh, as if steeling himself for what he had to say.

''One night, just before the guy comes to pick up the slips and the money, we got held up. Something like that never happened in the neighborhood. With all the hoodlums this was neutral territory. But here was this guy with a gun the size of a fifty-gallon drum, and a ski mask over his face. Well, Bobby Dee didn't believe there was a hold up. He thinks we made it up to steal his money. So, he sends one of his messengers to see me. I'm not there. It's early in the day, and I'm making a delivery. We had a big lunch order to deliver that took me and the kid I had working for me. When we got back, the place is broken up and Angela is hurt and bleeding. The messenger Bobby Dee sent was too eager, I guess. She died in the hospital. I knew I couldn't get close enough to Bobby Dee to kill the bastard—not with all his bodyguards. So I did what I could to hurt him.''

Benny leaned forward toward Peter. ''I handle problems by preparing for them. I got to know more about this Cuban guy, because they may get him to come after me instead of sending one of their own. There's always a little bit of cooperation to keep the peace among these guys. Sometimes it's best to deal with the locals 'cause they know their way around.

"And I don't know how to go about this without I bring attention to me also. That could make it worse, if the Cuban or locals start to take notice of me. Might do some checking on their own, find me out, and sell me to Bobby Dee." Benny shook his head. He realized how he sounded, and how he felt.

"I know I'm sounding paranoid. Maybe I am. After fourteen years of looking out, I could be making this bigger than it is. But if I know more about this guy, it might give me the edge if things go crazy. I mean, this guy might already be nosing around looking for me. Having trouble because all us old guys look alike."

Benny looked hard at Peter. "You're the only one I've ever told about this. Maybe I'm getting old. But I need your help bad."

Peter threw down the last of his Scotch, and felt the fire trace its way into his stomach. He regretted coming to this crazy place. He toyed with the empty glass in his hand. "You have given me the upper hand with this information. What I know of you negates your threat to accuse me of the theft of the jewelry. I have no reason to help you now."

Benny grinned. "Wrong, Slick. I didn't get this far being stupid. You blab about me, I got the government to take me out of here and find me a new place and a new name. Who you got? You'll be inside the walls a long time complaining to your lawyer."

Peter had to grin in spite of himself. "You're a piece of work, Benny."

"Yeah."

"I have one question," Peter said. "How did you get

the government to pay the bills on a place like this?"

"I threw in a lot of Bobby Dee's money."

Peter went back to his apartment tired and depressed. The whole world was churning around him, and he was being pushed from all sides. He undressed, slipped on a silk robe, poured himself a snifter of Amaretto, and sat in the chair looking out at the lake at night. It was a pretty, serene view. Not like what was happening to him. He was sitting there in the dark looking out at the moonlight reflecting off the lake, and sipping the Amaretto, thinking how much of Benny's story he didn't believe. He was still sitting pondering when there was a knock on the door. Peter turned on a lamp in the living room and answered the door. It was Benny.

"What is it now, Benny?" He'd had enough of this man for one night.

"Slick, I'm sorry but I got to get something off my chest."

"Now?"

"Now."

Peter sighed. "C'mon in."

Benny came in, closed the door behind him, and walked into the living room. He sat on the sofa. Peter went back to the chair he had been sitting in. "What is it, Benny?"

"Look, I'm not a bad guy. After you left I didn't feel right. Angela was whispering to me, if you know what I mean. There are some things I gotta clear up here. So, just listen and then you do what you want. First, I wouldn't lie to the cops about you taking Marjorie's jewelry. I know I threatened you with that. But I couldn't do it. I think even the cops would suspect that you wouldn't be that stupid, to come here, spend a lot of money contracting to live here, then rob somebody. But, anyway, I wouldn't do it. It's just that I need your help bad, and I was desperate. You understand, don't you?''

Peter nodded. Suddenly he felt affection for the little old man.

"And I lied to you about killing that guy who came to do me. Well, I didn't lie. I just let you think what wasn't true. I never killed anybody in my life. I was trying to scare you with that. The way it happened, this guy comes up to me on the street at night. He's wearing one of them raincoats. He says to me he's got a message from Bobby Dee. A young guy, too big for himself. I says, oh yeah, Bobby Dee. I look like a broken man, my head low and like that. I ask him how he found me, and he tells me about the man on the inside in the FBI. Oh, I says. Then he opens his coat and reaches for the gun in his belt. I shoved him, caught him by surprise, and the gun went off still in his belt. Shot himself in the leg, and must have broken a bone or something because he went down. I ran like hell. Next day I read in the paper how they found this guy who shot himself in the leg, opened an artery, and bled to death.

"That's all I got to tell you. If you don't want to help me, that's okay. But I couldn't let you lose any sleep because of my bullshit.'' Then he got up and went to the door. "You think about it, and tell me tomorrow what you decide.'' He opened the door and left.

Peter sat and watched Benny leave. Suddenly he liked that skinny old man. The man had had Peter by the throat, and he let him go. Because he's a not a bad guy, he'd said. *What a strange creature is the human,* Peter thought.

CHAPTER

9

The next morning Peter woke early and laid in bed for awhile thinking that this was much better than a rocker on the porch. He had been prepared for a quiet retirement, sitting around looking at the sky. He had pictured himself playing golf in the sun; even though he wasn't a golfer. It was the way retirement was portrayed, and it made a nice picture in his head. His strengths, however, were in the cocktail lounge and dinner party circuit. The world of the rich and bejeweled. He realized he had been expecting an endless, wonderful vacation with a lot of sighing at sunsets and carefree days. He wondered now if that was at all possible or realistic. Life had to have its ups and downs, even on vacation. It was true that right now he was in a mess, but he'd been through others much worse and handled them successfully. Why not this one? Things would somehow work out. And Coral Sands might have its eccentrics, but what had that to do with his enjoying his life? Nothing is ever all bad. It was simply a matter of one's point of view. The glass was either half empty or half full. He decided he'd look at the glass as half full. Maybe then the day would appear differently

to him. With that decision, he got up, shaved, dressed, and
went downstairs to the dining room for breakfast.

Eleanor, Betty, and Benny were huddled at one table near
the window. Chris stood at their table pouring orange juice
into the glasses before them. There were only a few other
people in the dining room. Peter walked to the table.
Eleanor was sparkling in a sun-yellow blouse and white
pleated skirt. It made him feel good to see her.

"Good morning," Eleanor said, giving him a pleasant
smile. *He is certainly handsome,* Eleanor thought. If she
couldn't have David Niven, this was close enough. He had
the looks and that elegant charm. What more could she ask?

"Well," Benny said. "Thought you'd sleep even later
today after our late night last night."

"Oh, it's so good you're here," Betty said, tingling with
excitement. "I told them you would come."

"Yes, she did," Benny said.

Chris smiled. "Good morning, Mr. Benington." He
raised the pitcher and poured orange juice in the glass in
front of Peter.

Peter nodded a greeting to each of them, and sat down
at the table. "Losing at poker makes me hungry. I can't
sleep when I'm hungry."

"I have some remedies for not being able to sleep,"
Eleanor said, playfully seductive.

"You must show them to me sometime." Peter grinned.

"If you're lucky." She smiled.

"Not many people eat breakfast," Peter said, looking
around the empty dining room.

"It is obvious you haven't seen the newspaper," Benny
said. "This place has a crazy murderer on the loose. Everybody's scared the guy is poisoning the food." He looked
at Chris. "Should make your job easier for awhile."

"Raymond, the cook, is near a breakdown after reading

the paper. Everybody's afraid the cops'll be trying to blame them," Chris said. "This job has turned into something I didn't expect. When Carlos is better, I'm going to find a job working on boats or something. The people here are nice, but I can't handle all this dying." Then he managed a weak smile. "I'm sorry. I'm supposed to be cheerful. You want to order?"

They gave him their breakfast orders, and Chris went away.

Eleanor said, "Betty was telling us that she spoke to Eugene last night, and he said that Marjorie was murdered for her money."

"Yes," Betty interjected excitedly, "and the only person who would benefit from her money was her daughter."

Peter was already having trouble holding on to his view of the glass being half full. "How do you talk to Eugene?" he asked, taking a sip of his orange juice.

"Ouija board mostly," Betty said. "Sometimes, if I sit quietly and call to him, too. But it is usually the Ouija board. Eugene and I used to use the Ouija board a lot. He told me if he died before me, I could contact him with the Ouija board."

"And last night?"

"I used the Ouija board."

"What exactly did he say?"

"Well, I asked him if Marjorie was murdered. He said 'yes.' "

"Yes or no. That's fifty/fifty on the right answer," Benny said, with a shrug.

Betty went on, ignoring Benny, "Then I asked him why she was murdered. And he said 'money.' "

"Of course, it's either money or love," Benny said, with a little sarcasm in his tone. "Again, fifty/fifty odds on the answer."

"Did you ask him who murdered her?" Peter said.

"No," Betty said, her eyes wide. "Because who else would get her money except her daughter? And we all know her daughter and Marjorie didn't get along at all."

Benny was getting annoyed at this conversation about some talking dead guy. "Well, there's her daughter's husband?" He drank some orange juice, and it dribbled onto his chin. He frowned and wiped it off with his napkin.

"Oh my," Betty said, her hand to her mouth. "I hadn't thought of that." For a moment she thought that over. "You did tell us he was having money problems with his business. Yes, it could be him." She made a *tsk*ing sound of annoyance with her tongue. "Eugene never volunteers any information when it's important—like this. I always have to ask him really specific questions. I hate it when he does that."

Benny said, wiping orange juice off his chin once again, "And there are all the people who he owes money to. And who knows what sort of debt Madeliene has. The chain of money goes out like a pyramid. Eugene has to do better than that."

"You know," Eleanor said, "Marjorie did complain about not feeling well before she ate any breakfast."

"The bread pudding her daughter made," Betty said. "She said she didn't feel too good after she ate at her daughter's house that night."

"That's right," Benny said, wiping more orange juice from his chin. "She ate with her daughter's family the night before she died. And Georgie came here with more bread pudding the next day. She told him that it was her favorite, and ate so much it made her feel sick. God. Done in by poisoned raisins." He groaned with obvious exaggeration. He was swallowing none of this.

Betty said, her expression very serious, "I think we

should go to that policeman and tell him all this.''

"What's the matter, Benny need a straw?" Eleanor said with a smirk, noticing him wiping his chin yet again.

"Damn. I keep getting orange juice on my chin." They all looked at him. He twirled the glass slowly in the light. Then he started giggling. "I've been had. This is one of them trick glasses." The more he thought of it, the more he began to laugh. Trying to keep his hand steady, he gently turned the glass to pour, but kept the juice from the edge. Drops of juice dripped out from the pattern.

They all smiled at him, mostly because his laughter was contagious.

"I still think we should tell the police," Betty said, getting back to it.

"Great," Benny said, "tell the cops that your dead husband told you all this? Get real, Betty."

"Is that what Eugene told you to do?" Peter asked. He was trying to take Eugene seriously, but it wasn't easy.

"No," she said. "When I asked him what I should do, he said, 'Miss Marple.' Heck," she said, with a pout, "I can't do what she does."

Peter said, "Perhaps there is an influence here from the television. Murder is not as common as the television dramas portray it."

Two gruesome pictures flashed into Eleanor's mind. Two murdered men from her past. She shivered with the cold of remembering, and pushed the images back into the dark corner.

Peter said, "I think we are jumping to unrealistic conclusions here."

"But, Eugene told me." Betty insisted. "Eugene never lies to me. Sometimes he teases me, but he never lies."

"Did Eugene tell you about the Home being for sale?" Benny said, rolling his eyes. He couldn't believe she was taking all this so seriously. He thought it was all baloney.

"No," Betty frowned. "He wasn't very talkative last night."

"You mean that's it?" Benny said with a mocking grin. "No more news from the other side?"

"Oh, there was something else, but I don't know what it means." She took a piece of paper from the pocket of her dress, unfolded it, and handed it to Benny. "I wrote it down because I didn't understand it. Eugene never does that—give me messages that make no sense. Maybe there was interference like you get with the television. You think that's possible, Eleanor?"

"Betty, I don't know. Anything's possible, I guess."

"I don't know what this says," Benny said, peering at the piece of paper in his hands. "Just a bunch of letters: E, U, S, T, A, Q, U, I, O." He gave Peter a questioning look.

Peter shrugged. "I have no idea. A name? Some type of code?"

"What about the other two deaths?" Eleanor said. "How do they figure in this?"

"Well," Benny said, warming to this, "last night Alice said that sometimes a killer does more than one person to hide the real victim."

"You think Madeliene killed them all?" Betty said, shocked. "How could she be so cold?"

With a shrug, and sarcasm slipping into his voice—it wasn't easy to hold on to the belief—Peter said, "They say, after the first time it becomes easier."

Eleanor gave Peter a warning look. Benny pointed to Eleanor and said to Peter, "Watch out for her elbows. I think she's got a black belt in elbows."

"How would she be able to do that? Kill the others?"

Eleanor said. "She couldn't simply walk in here. She'd have to pass Grace."

"No easy job, I tell you," Benny said.

Chris showed up with a tray of food and placed their breakfast orders in front of them on the table. "Enjoy your breakfast, and your day." Chris smiled and stepped away.

They sat looking at the food before them on the table.

Betty said, cautiously, "I should have asked Eugene about the food being poisoned."

"What is it now, Manuel?" Jessie Cummings asked. She was ready for another bad day. This morning she had put on a white blouse with pastel shades of greens, reds, and yellows in delicate flowing designs, and a tan skirt. Something to brighten her mood in preparation for the day. The newspaper lay in front of her on her desk. She had just finished reading the article in the paper on the "house of death"—a quip in the article. Just what she needed to lift her mood, she thought sarcastically. And now here was Manuel standing in the doorway to her office.

"I know, I say I won't bother you no more, but . . ." Manuel gave her a helpless shrug. "Is now glasses, too." He ticked them off on his fingers: "Wine glasses, water glasses, juice glasses, rocks glasses, goblets." He shook his head in despair. "So much is missing. These must be happening a long time."

"Or our thief is in a hurry," Jessie said.

"Maybe his restaurant is opening soon," Manuel said, straight-faced.

Jessie smiled. "How about you put together a list of all the things I'll need to order? I've already ordered the spoons, so, you can leave them off. Unless there are more missing."

"Yes," he said, "I will do that. But I think, maybe, you

take your time to order. Not many eat this morning." He pointed to the newspaper. "There is rumor the food is poison."

"Oh, damn," she said, suddenly weary.

The telephone rang on her desk. With a sigh, she picked it up. "Jessie Cummings."

"Detective Ralph Ardley here, *Ms.* Cummings." Again he stressed the Ms. "I saw the newspaper this morning, and I thought I'd let you know that we got the results back from toxicology on the other two deaths. Poison, also. No chance of a mass suicide. You do have a murderer on the loose. I'll have people over there today questioning the staff. Be on the lookout for reporters."

"Thanks for the call, *Detective*," Jessie said, stressing "Detective" back at him, and hung up. She looked at the clock. Ten-thirty and the day was in the toilet already.

She looked back to Manuel. "Tell the rest of the kitchen staff that the police will be here to talk to them today."

Manuel raised his eyes to the sky in a plea for strength, then he turned and left.

Grace came in with a telephone message. "This guy called while you were on the phone. A Toby Williams. He's a reporter for the *Herald*. Wants to come over and talk with you." Grace raised an eyebrow and gave a slight shrug with her shoulder. "I told him you'd call him when you got in."

"Thanks, Grace."

"I don't think it will stop him, though. And I expect we'll get a visit from the TV news as well."

"Not enough ugly news around?" Jessie said, shaking her head. "I'd appreciate it if you could keep them out of the way, and tell them nothing. I don't want the residents harassed by some hungry reporters. I'm sure they've got enough on their minds right now without being grilled by the news."

"I'll do my best," Grace said.

"Recruit any of the staff you need to keep the situation under control. No news crews in the Home. Give them Jacobson's number. If they want a statement, it'll have to come from him."

"He's going to love that." Grace grinned.

"Maybe it'll keep him off my back for awhile."

"Excuse me?" Peter said.

Jessie looked over to the door. Peter and Benny were standing there. "Yes?"

"Could we have a word with you?" Peter asked. For a moment Jessie wished Peter were a little younger. He was damn good looking and very suave, and there was something very attractive about his English accent.

Jessie looked at Grace. "I think we're finished here. Right?"

Grace nodded. "I'll keep you updated on events," she said, and left.

Peter came over to the desk and placed a cup of coffee in front of Jessie. "We thought you might enjoy some coffee." Peter smiled. *Laying on the charm,* she thought, *and he does it so well.*

"Please sit down," she said. "The day has barely begun, and already I could use a break."

Peter and Benny sat in the two chairs facing the desk.

"So, what can I do for you?" she smiled, and felt herself flirting with Peter.

"Rumors are flying," Peter said, "and we thought we'd come to the source of truth."

"Rumors are flying in normal times," she said. "I can imagine what they must be like now." She sipped the coffee, and was surprised at how good it tasted. "The least I can do is give you the facts. What particular rumors are you concerned about?''

Benny spoke up. ''You got any buyers for the Home?''

''God,'' she said. ''The rumor mill doesn't miss a trick. Sometimes I think my office is bugged.'' She let out a deep sigh. ''Well, the answer is no. That's as much as I know now. Jacobson hasn't confided in me on this. I had to learn about this from someone who came in here the other day looking for a place for his mother.'' She shrugged a grin. ''The man said he might be interested in buying the place— and I'd be working for him. I didn't give it much thought, at first. After I saw him at Marjorie's funeral, I checked with Jacobson. He didn't say yes, and he didn't say no.''

''The Cuban?'' Benny asked.

Jessie gave him a puzzled look and shook her head. ''Who are you talking about?''

''There was a Cuban man here the day Marjorie died,'' Peter said. ''Alice Chomseky almost knocked him over on her way to a performance. And we saw him at Marjorie's funeral, standing off in the distance.''

She nodded. ''Mr. Vasquez, yes, that was him.''

''I was wondering if you could give us Mr. Vasquez's address.'' Peter kept talking before she could raise a protest. ''We've been discussing the possibility of the residents actually buying Coral Sands. And we'd like to discuss with him his offer and to what extent we could reach some sort of agreement. He may be willing to settle for a minor interest in Coral Sands, with the residents owning a major interest.''

Jessie Cummings looked at Peter with surprise and admiration. Sometimes it was easy to forget that these old people had been the movers and shakers in society before they retired. Here were people who had worked the system and prospered.

"Well, his address is about all I can give you," she said. She got up from the chair, went over to the file cabinet, and pulled open the top drawer. She flipped through the file folders. "I really don't do more than ask the applicants for their address so I can reach them if we have something they might be interested in." She pulled out a folder and brought it back to her desk. "Screening on their financial picture is done at that time." She sat down and opened the folder. "Nine twenty-three Main Street in Sarasota," she read from the notes. "No phone number here. We don't usually ask for it."

"Nine hundred twenty-three Main Street," Peter repeated.

"Jessie"—it was Grace at the door—"I'm sorry to interrupt, but that Detective Ardley is here with a bunch of policemen. He wants to talk to you."

Jessie's shoulders sagged. "And the day crashes on."

Peter and Benny rose from their chairs, each anxious to avoid Ardley.

Jessie looked at them as they moved to the door. "If you guys find out anything, I'd appreciate it if you could share it with me."

The two men left Jessie's office and walked past Detective Ardley and four men who Peter knew were obviously policemen.

"Good to see you, Mr. Benington," Ardley said, as they walked by. He was giving Peter a look like a vulture watching his meal ripen. Peter ignored the man and headed across the lobby to the coffee alcove. Benny was right with him.

Benny said, in a low voice, "He looks anxious to get your ass."

"He'll have to take his place in line," Peter said. Though, he thought, right now Ardley was at the head of the line.

"I got to hand it to you, Slick," Benny said. "You really know how to run the field. That story about us buying the place was terrific. Jumping on that as if it wasn't just that instant made up."

Peter gave Benny a confident grin. Peter's profession had required being able to lie in an instant. And he was very good at what he did. "Well, you have your address."

"Yeah," Benny said, "thanks. I owe you one."

"I hope it gets you what you want," Peter said.

Benny took hold of Peter's arm and stopped him. "Look, Slick, there's something I've been meaning to ask you. Now, don't say anything until you hear me out."

Peter nodded.

"I want you to come to dinner at the house of a friend of mine." The words were coming out carefully, as if Benny were groping for them. "You see . . . well . . . Caroline's been after me to meet some of my friends. I guess I haven't brought her around because I didn't want to take a ribbing from you guys. Anyway, I promised Caroline I'd bring a couple of people to dinner tomorrow night. I already asked Eleanor, and she said okay. So, how about it, Slick? You want to come, too?"

"Who else will be there?" Peter said.

"Nobody. Just you and Eleanor. And please don't tell anyone else about it. Especially Betty. I don't want to hurt her feelings, but if Betty comes, then along comes Eugene. I'm trying to impress Caroline, not scare her."

"I'd be happy to go," Peter said, thinking it would be a good way to move a little closer to Eleanor. Perhaps take her someplace afterward where they could talk alone. Let things move more naturally, rather than have it look like he's mounting a major assault.

"Good," Benny said, relieved. "We'll leave at seven tomorrow night."

"Good afternoon, gentlemen." It was Mr. Petersen, stopping by them in the middle of the lobby. "Good to see you again, Benny and"—looking at Peter, he hesitated, searching his memory—"Peter Benington, that's it. Yes, I met you the other day in the dining room."

"Yes," Peter said, surprised at the man's memory when Petersen couldn't remember who he himself was each day. "You are?"

"Holmes," Petersen said. "Sherlock Holmes. You asked for me the other day."

Benny looked at Peter. Yes, Peter thought, when he had seen Fred Astaire coming down the hall. This is getting crazier.

"So, may I ask what it is you need from me?" Holmes said.

Jesus, Peter thought. *What the hell do I do now?* "Well, yes. I did, sir."

Benny said, throwing a glance at Peter, "There's been a couple of murders. We thought you could help with them."

"A couple?" Holmes said. "You are mistaken, Benny. Four is the exact number."

"Four!" Benny said.

"Yes. Poor Mrs. Walden was just found by her husband up in their rooms." Petersen turned to Peter. "I am sorry, but until the police request my assistance, I can not interfere. You do understand?"

"Now Elizabeth?" Benny said to himself.

"Yes, I do, Mr. Holmes," Peter said, going along with it. "I will try to persuade them to seek your help. And I appreciate your answering my plea for help."

Holmes frowned at Peter. "Interesting accent, sir. If I may be so bold, it does need more practice. You have mixed up a number of accents from various parts of England. Additionally, there is the unmistaken undertone of

American English—New York City. Brooklyn, most probably, though there are too many regional accents in that
part of New York to be more precise. It is a good effort,
but you must develop a better ear for the language before
you attempt to imitate it.'' Benny looked wide eyed at Peter. Peter was at a loss for words. ''Well,'' Holmes said,
''I will be available, should you succeed in persuading the
police to seek my help. Good day to you both.'' He nodded,
then hurried off.

   ''What the hell was that all about?'' Benny said, suspicious. ''Brooklyn?''

   ''Benny, let's be serious about this. The man is mentally
ill, remember? He is pretending to be Sherlock Holmes, and
he has just given us a performance. What was it you said
to Betty earlier—'get real?' '' Peter thought he would have
to watch out for Mr. Sherlock Holmes in the future. ''Now,
let us join the women for lunch.''

CHAPTER
10

Peter and Benny joined Betty and Eleanor, and told them the news about Emily Walden being found dead. Eleanor had said it was probably for the best, considering the state of her Alzheimer's and poor Ted's frail condition. Betty just sighed and shook her head sadly. "How many friends can I lose like this?" she said.

The mourners' lunch for Corrine Medford started at eleven. Eleanor and Peter went into the dining room about eleven-thirty. Benny had begged off, saying he had something to do. And then he had done a strange thing, he had invited Betty to join him. She was thrilled, and didn't ask where they were going. Eleanor told Benny to give his girlfriend her regards. Benny made a face at her, Betty giggled, and they left.

There weren't many people attending the lunch. Not a good showing for Corrine Medford. Peter figured it would be that way until the food was no longer under suspicion of being poisoned. Eleanor took a bowl of fruit chunks from the buffet table. For her girlish figure, she told Peter. Peter scooped some of the salads on his plate, took a fork and followed Eleanor to a table by the window. It gave a nice view of the swimming pool and the palm trees by the lake.

After they were seated, Peter said, "What do you know about Benny?"

"Benny? He's all right. He's a rough cut, but the edges aren't sharp, if you know what I mean. As to his history, I don't know much. His wife was killed many years ago. And he came here alone. I got that much from Grace. I think he was born in some tough neighborhood in Brooklyn." She smiled. "I guess his accent gives him away on that." She picked up a chunk of melon with her spoon and put it in her mouth.

The mention of accents brought Sherlock Holmes to mind, but Peter didn't want to discuss accents. He forked some egg salad into his mouth and looked out the window at the view. Certainly looked like paradise. After a moment he looked back to Eleanor. "What did he do for a living, do you know?"

"Oh, yes. He was a mechanic of some kind. I don't remember what kind exactly."

Well, Peter thought, *at least Benny didn't tell her the same story he told me.* Maybe. Unless he swore her to secrecy, too. Benny's story bothered Peter. Too much Hollywood in it. Benny was definitely a puzzle.

"Geez." Eleanor grimaced, and pulled the piece of melon from her mouth. Then her expression changed and she giggled. "What a funny feeling—chewing on a piece of melon that turns out to be rubber."

"The joker strikes again," Peter said, and chuckled.

She nodded, still giggling as she placed the piece of rubber melon on the table.

"It is too bad that Benny is not here," Peter said. "He would be in stitches." He smiled at the thought of Benny laughing uncontrollably, holding his sides. The man sure knew how to enjoy himself. Then Peter told Eleanor about the card game and the deck of cards that had been slipped into the game. It brought a laughing smile to her face. "Do you think Benny is pulling off these stunts?" he said.

"I don't know. He sure laughs hard enough at them to be guilty."

Peter remembered Benny's fear last night when he talked about being hunted. Maybe there was a way to help Benny without really getting involved.

Eleanor noticed that Peter had been picking at his food with little interest. "Why don't we go outside by the pool and soak up some of the atmosphere?"

"Yes," he said, glad to be rid of the food. He wasn't sure it wasn't his imagination, but the food didn't taste right. "But let me meet you out there. I must go to my apartment and make a telephone call."

"Dad!" said the man at the other end of the line. "How're you doing? How's paradise?"

"It is just terrific, son," Peter said. *If you discount being a suspect in a jewel theft, and people dropping dead all around you.* "There has been sunshine since I arrived. I couldn't ask for a nicer place."

"Yeah. Guess that's why all the crooks end up down there to retire."

"You mean there aren't enough crooks up there to keep you police busy?"

"More than our share. But, hell, no crooks, no job."

"David, I have a favor to ask."

"Asking's not the problem. Favorable answers may be."

"There is an unsavory character down here I'd like to know more about. It is for a friend of mine. I was wondering if you could make inquiries with the Sarasota police? See what you can find out about him?"

"Living in the place with you?"

"No. He is not *mature* enough." Emphasis on the word "mature."

David laughed. "You mean he's not chronologically challenged, yet."

Peter smiled. "Yes."

"I'll see what I can do. You got any information on him?"

"His name is Vasquez. Address: Nine hundred twenty-three Main Street here in Sarasota. That's all I know."

"Got it. Okay, I'll get back to you. Maybe later this afternoon all right?"

"I will be here."

"What? No cavorting in paradise?"

"Well, there's this woman, you see . . ." He let the words hang.

David laughed. "My Dad. Doesn't waste any time."

"There's not much time left to waste." Peter laughed. "So many women, so little time."

"Just remember—safe sex, now."

Peter laughed. "You needn't worry about any brothers or sisters."

Still laughing, David said, "Enjoy, Dad. I'll get back to you."

They said their good-byes and hung up.

Peter spent a few minutes putting together piña coladas, dumped the mixture in a thermos, and grabbed two glasses from the cupboard. He left the room and headed for the elevator. In the lobby, he got off the elevator and walked across to the front desk. He wanted to tell Grace where he'd be should a call come in for him. As Peter approached the desk, Detective Ardley stepped out of Jessie Cummings's office, spotted Peter, and gave him a wicked smiled. Ardley raised a hand, finger and thumb extended like a gun, and pointed it at Peter. Then he brought his thumb down like the hammer of a gun, the smile still on the man's face. *Well,* Peter thought, *so much for the glass being half full.* Ardley then walked out the front door. Peter told Grace he'd be by the pool should a call come in, thanked her, and went out to meet Eleanor.

Eleanor was stretched out on a lounge chair in the shade of the striped awning along the wall at the far end of the pool area. The gazebo with Tweedledee and Tweedledum was just a short way beyond. Eleanor wore sunglasses, and her hair was splayed casually against the back of the chair. The sunlight made her body glow with its radiance. He thought she looked terrific and mysterious. Lauren Bacall in some spy thriller.

When she saw him Eleanor smiled and patted the empty lounge chair next to her. He sat in the chair and placed the thermos and glass on the small table between them. To the question in her eyes, he answered, "A little tropical refreshment." He opened the thermos, poured out two drinks, and offered her one. "Piña colada?"

She grinned and licked her lips. "Perfect," she said, taking the glass and tasting the drink. "Excellent. Thank you."

"The pleasure is mine, dear lady." Playful flirting was in his eyes and in his smile. He took a sip, the cold, delicious drink coating his throat. Then he stretched out on the lounge and looked at the sky crowded with white lumbering clouds. "Nice today."

"Yes," she sighed. "So peaceful here."

" 'A place where one can live one's life a full measure,' " he said, and then sighed. "Don't know who said that, but he had it right. It's what we all search for."

"Yes, and it's like that sometimes. The days move by slowly and gently, not disturbing, not tense, not in a rush."

"I guess I arrived at the wrong time."

"All things pass," she said, her voice far away.

They stayed like that, for a long time not speaking. Just sipping their drinks and taking in the peacefulness of the moment.

Tweedledee and Tweedledum came through the glass doors from the lobby onto the deck around the swimming pool, and slowly ambled their way past Eleanor and Peter. Sailor Hat was wearing a T-shirt that read: ROCKERS TOUGHEN THE WRONG END.

Gray Hair said "Heard they took the cook out of here in handcuffs."

"This the new cook?"

"Yep."

"His cooking wasn't all that bad that he should be arrested. Only four people died."

"Seems he was a wanted man."

"For what?"

"Sex crimes."

"What are they?"

"What are what?

"What are sex crimes?"

"You think my memory's any better than yours?"

At that point they were out of earshot on their way to the gazebo.

Eleanor turned away from the sky and looked at Peter. He certainly was a handsome man. And really a smooth character. She liked his gentle manner and cool approach to things. And his playful flirting with her. Being around him made her feel foolishly young again. He must have had no problem getting the attention of any woman he wanted. She wondered why he never married after his wife left him so many years ago?

Peter said, suddenly, "Did you hear that? They arrested the cook."

"Yes. I saw them take him away while you were gone. The man looked sad and broken."

"He was doing the poisoning?"

"I don't know. Grace said the police found he was wanted through his fingerprints. And they came and took him away. That's all she knew."

Maybe the food will taste better, he thought.

"There was a play I saw a long time ago, *Arsenic and Old Lace*, about two old ladies putting old men out of their misery by poisoning them," Eleanor said.

"Well, I don't see that here," Peter said. "There are plenty of other places where old people are more miserable and need that sort of help. Here you would put them out of their money, not their misery."

"Yes," she said, "and Eugene said Marjorie was murdered for her money."

"Please, let's leave Eugene out of this," Peter said, rolling his eyes.

Eleanor turned her attention to the sky once again. After a moment she said, "Grace said there were reporters from the newspaper and a television-news crew outside. When the police took Raymond away, the news people took off after them. So, it's safe to leave without being mobbed by the press." Eleanor shrugged. "I told her we didn't even know they were out there to begin with." She took a deep breath, and sighed. "Mr. Walden was in the lobby earlier crying like a baby, Grace said. She felt so bad for the man—to lose his wife like that."

"You were a busy girl while I was gone," Peter said.

They let the conversation end and the peacefulness of the day come over them once again. They were quiet for a long time before Peter spoke. "Why aren't you worried about being poisoned?"

Eleanor said, her voice far away again, "You don't seem to be overly concerned. The cool, calm Englishman. Are you worried?"

"Well," he said, "I was not at first."

"Yes," she said, "me, too. That's why I had the fruit salad for lunch. I figured it would be less likely to be tampered with."

Peter said, "Maybe we should do what the others are doing—eat out, until this is all settled?"

"Maybe," she said, and left it at that.

Walter Innes walked over to them, leaning heavily on his cane. He was dressed in gray shorts and a blue short-sleeved shirt. It was the hat—a multicolored fisherman's hat—that made him look the part of the retiree in Florida. That and the white jogging shoes and blue mirror sunglasses.

"I was wondering," Walter said, "if you'd care to give an old doctor some company."

"Give us a break," Eleanor said, with a laugh. "Park it." She indicated the chair next to her.

Walter smiled and, leaning on his cane, carefully sat on the lounge chair the other side of Eleanor.

"That drink you're holding sure looks good," Walter said.

"That old man stuff will get you a seat, but no drink," Eleanor smiled.

"No respect for one's elders," Walter said, putting a good deal of mock sadness in the tone of his voice.

"All right"—she chuckled—"but you'll need a glass."

"Well"—he grinned—"look what I have here." From his pocket he pulled a metal ring that telescoped into a cup. "I am always prepared."

Still laughing, Eleanor poured him a piña colada from the thermos. With his other hand on the cane as if for support, he moved the cup carefully—his hand trembling—to his mouth and took a sip. He licked his lips. "Delicious."

"Don't look at me. Peter made it," Eleanor said.

Walter raised the cup in a toast to Peter. "A man who can mix drinks, knows jewelry, and plays terrible poker. My kind of friend."

Peter grinned. "You did not take away any money from the game."

"Ah, that is true. But a loser loves company." Walter sipped the drink again, and sighed with satisfaction.

Peter said, "Being a doctor . . ."

Walter Innes interrupted, "Former doctor, now retired. I don't give out medical advice, free or otherwise."

"What do you know about poisons?" Peter said.

"That the world is full of them. Only one percent of all plant life is edible, that many insects and other creatures can kill a man. Many poisons are found in the human body in concentrations small enough not to kill. That it is remarkable mankind has survived at all. And now there are a number of man-made poisons, as if nature hadn't given us enough already. Do you wish to hear more?"

"That police detective said arsenic and strychnine?"

"Ah. You are referring to our in-house murderer." He pursed his lips in thought, and searched his memory. "Well, they are both common drugs, readily available if one is bent on obtaining them for some deadly purpose. Highly toxic. A minute amount is all that it takes to destroy a person. Arsenic causes severe gastric distress and all the symptoms associated with such a condition. The person enters a convulsive state and dies." He hesitated, and frowned at the text he was searching in his memory. "Strychnine. Well, now, the drug causes extremely severe spasms where the victim is literally thrown around. And rigor sets in immediately after death." He shrugged, and sipped his drink. "That is the extent of my immediate knowledge."

"What about quantity?" Peter said.

"And taste?" Eleanor said.

"Very small amounts of either drug will kill you. A few drops or so." With his drink he pointed to Eleanor. "But you do have a point there about the taste. They are bitter pills. To poison someone you would obviously have to disguise the flavor."

"You mean, mix it with a large quantity of food?" Peter said.

"Or drink," Walter said. "But not so large. For example, grapefruit juice is a bit tart in its own right. I would assume, these poisons would go unnoticed mixed in."

"How soon after taking it would they die?" Eleanor said.

"Well, that depends on how much was given, and how much food was eaten. I would say between twenty minutes or so to a number of hours. Even a day or more." Walter sipped the drink and smacked his lips. "This is very good. Have I paid for my drink?"

Eleanor and Peter smiled and nodded.

"Good. Now I may enjoy the rest of this wonderful concoction in peace." He sat back in the lounge chair, sipped the drink and sighed. Peter was left to ponder the odd taste of the food he had just eaten at lunch.

When Benny and Betty returned shortly after three they found Eleanor and Peter still by the pool. Walter Innes was sleeping quietly in the chair next to Eleanor. Benny wore a serious frown, while Betty was bubbling with excitement.

"I felt like a detective," Betty said in a gush. "It was so exciting."

Benny gave her a look, then said to Peter and Eleanor, "That address was a restaurant, Pancho's, serves Mexican and Spanish stuff."

Betty said, "I had some really delicious food, but I don't know what it was called. Benny ordered for me."

Benny shrugged. "I just pointed at the menu. I wasn't interested in the food. It was Vasquez that I was looking for."

"It was a nice place," Betty said. "All sorts of things around hanging on the walls, sombreros, blankets, painted dolls, and things like that."

Peter raised an eyebrow at Benny. "You didn't wear that hat, did you?"

Betty said, "He left it in the car before we went in the restaurant."

Benny shrugged. "I didn't want to take the chance he'd recognize me with the hat. He was in the Home that morning, and I did see him at the funeral."

Eleanor said, "Who?"

Peter said, "The Cuban we saw at Richard Allan's business." Then to Benny, "Was he there?"

"Not at first. I thought we'd have to eat again, because he didn't show. I was even thinking of asking the bartender where Vasquez was. But I thought that one over, and decided against it. Didn't want to draw attention to myself, if you know what I mean?"

Eleanor said, "What's this all about? Why were you doing this?"

Peter looked to Benny to explain.

"Let's just say it's a hunch I got. Anyway, the guy finally shows up after the third cup of coffee. Comes waltzing in like he owns the place. He waves to the bartender, the waiters. And the maître d'—I thought he was gonna piss his pants falling all over the guy."

Peter said, "Maybe he does own the place."

"Yeah," Benny said. "But that's not the big news. It was the guy who was with him that set me back in my chair. Herman, the muscles who takes steno at Richard Allan's place."

Peter frowned. "Allan's assistant?"

"Yeah," Benny said. "Walks in behind the man, struttin' his muscles around like a bodyguard. Kinda makes you wonder, don't it?"

"Curious," Peter said. "Did he recognize you?"

"Muscles? Naw. He was too busy posing and suckin' up to Vasquez to notice anything."

Eleanor was patently annoyed. "You guys want to tell me what this is all about? I hate sitting here listening to this crap and not knowing."

Benny said, "There's an odd coincidence here that's getting odder. I mean, when you think about it. Like, Richard Allan's mother-in-law dies and leaves his wife a bunch of money, which he needs badly for his business. Timing seems to be good on that one. And this Vasquez guy shows his face here the day Marjorie dies. Then he's at the funeral. Then he's at Richard Allan's place when we went there. And now, the guy who works for Allan shows up like a buddy to Vasquez."

Eleanor said, incredulously, "You think Richard Allan arranged to have Marjorie killed for her money?"

"Seven hundred grand is a lot of reasons," Benny said. "I knew guys'd do it for a lot less."

"But, Richard Allan? Georgie's father?" Eleanor said. "You know this sounds a little crazy." But she admitted to herself that she, too, used to know people who would do it for a lot less.

"Well," Betty said, speaking with absolute conviction, "Eugene said Marjorie had been killed for her money."

Peter said, "And the police are treating this as a homicide."

"And"—Walter Innes opened his eyes—"No one would choose arsenic and strychnine as a method of suicide."

They had forgotten he was there. Now they all looked at him.

"They are painful ways to die," Walter said. "Anyone in their right mind would use something more gentle, like narcotics. Sleeping pills, for instance. Much easier to get a prescription from any doctor. And there is no discomfort."

"Then how does this Vasquez person fit into all this?" Eleanor asked.

"I don't know," Benny said, "but he's a shady character. And now that we know he's got a man sittin' at Richard Allan's door, it's a sure thing he figures in somehow."

"Poor Georgie," Walter Innes said. "I really like that child. He's . . ."

Peter didn't hear any more of what Walter was saying because he saw Grace coming through the doorway looking at him. She pointed at him, and then held her fist to her ear indicating a phone call. Peter nodded, excused himself, and headed toward Grace. He followed her back to the front desk, and she pointed at the telephone on the table in the corner of the lobby next to a stuffed love seat. Peter went over, sat down and picked up the receiver.

"David?" he said.

"Hey, Dad," David said, at the other end. "You score yet with that lady friend?"

Peter grinned. "If I did, do you think I would be answering this telephone call?"

"Not a minuteman, huh?"

"Love, like fine wine, should be sipped and savored, not

tossed down the throat in one gulp," Peter said. "You young people have much to learn."

"Young people?" David said. "Trying to make me feel good?"

"If that's all it takes, you're easy."

"All right, I give up." David laughed. "I got the information you wanted on that Vasquez character. And he is a real character. Unsavory was the correct word. The guy is a major player in a minor town. Extortion, prostitution, loan-sharking, the list goes on. Like most guys like this, the cops have a hard time getting anything to stick on him. Hope your friend isn't doing business with this guy?"

"I will definitely advise him against it." Peter hesitated before asking the next question, "Do you think this Vasquez is into killing people?"

"It's a tough life if he isn't."

"I guess that's true," Peter said.

"Anyway, the address you gave me is a restaurant—Pancho's, where he holds court. He beds down in a house on Anna Maria Island. Address is Five hundred twenty-three Gulfview Drive. From what the detective told me, a nice piece of real estate. The guy's called T. T., short for 'Tough Tony' Vasquez. The detective said he earned the name. Nobody fools with this character. He's been linked with a lot of ugly stuff. His real first name the detective I spoke to couldn't pronounce, and I can't either. Let me spell it for you: E, U, S, T, A, Q, U, I, O."

Peter felt a chill run up his back.

CHAPTER

11

"Guy goes to the doctor and tells him he needs help with his love life. The doctor tells him to run ten miles a day. Two weeks later the guy calls the doctor. The doctor says, 'How's your love life?' The guy says, 'I don't know, I'm a hundred forty miles from home.'"

Benny was laughing so hard, holding his sides, there were tears in his eyes. Betty was giggling, and Eleanor was smiling and chuckling. Walter Innes was stoic. Petersen stood before them like a man on stage. Benny had seated himself in the lounge chair Peter had left, and Betty had perched herself on the end of the chair.

Peter walked toward the group after saying good-bye to his son. Peter was not in a laughing mood.

"A woman calls the police department. 'I have a sex maniac in my apartment. You can pick him up in the morning.'"

Peter came up beside Petersen. "Henny, I have to talk to your audience, if you don't mind."

Petersen looked at him with innocent eyes. "Of course. Of course." Then to the audience, "I don't want to use up all my material, folks. So, I'll end this performance with the fact that I take my wife everywhere, but she always finds her way home." He smiled, gave a short bow. "You've been a wonderful audience. Exit stage left." And he walked away.

It took a few moments for Benny's laughing to settle to snorting and giggling.

Walter Innes said, indicating Benny, "No matter how many times he hears those jokes, he still breaks up."

"I just received news from my son," Peter said. Benny was still giggling. "He's a detective with the Newark New Jersey Police Department. I called him earlier to see what he could find out about our Mr. Vasquez. Well, he confirmed that the man is a bad character. He is involved in loan sharking, extortion, and prostitution among other things. His cohorts call him T. T. which is short for Tough Tony. But his real name is spelled: E, U, S, T, A, Q, U, I, O."

Benny stopped giggling and frowned at Peter. "This some kind of joke, Slick?"

Betty said, "See, I told you that Eugene never lies to me."

Eleanor shook her head. "Weird."

Walter Innes looked confused. Eleanor told him about Betty's conversation with Eugene. He nodded with understanding.

Peter then said, "I think we can say with some certainty that Richard Allan is mixed up with our friend T. T. somehow. Just how, I can only speculate. Richard Allan told us that he had gone deeply into debt, borrowing from everyone until there was no one left. Vasquez is into loan-sharking. Possibly Richard borrowed from him when all other sources went dry."

Benny said, "And then killed his mother-in-law to get

the money he needed to get Vasquez off his back?''

"Or he had Vasquez do it," Eleanor said. "But it will be months before Marjorie's estate has been through probate and he can get his hands on the money."

Walter Innes said, "Could be as little as a month, depending on how complex the estate is. And how good the attorney is doing the probate and settling the taxes. Some of the money could be available before probate."

"What about the other deaths?" Betty asked.

"Let's deal with one death at a time. They may be related, then again, they may not," Peter said.

"How did this Vasquez person kill Marjorie?" Betty said.

"You mean, how did he administer the poison. Well," Peter said, "they took the cook out in handcuffs. Possibly Vasquez had him do it?"

Benny said, "Don't forget the bread pudding, Slick."

"Yes," Peter said, "that would implicate Richard Allan directly. But all this speculation isn't going to get anywhere."

"Poor Georgie," Walter Innes said. "That kid deserves better. A kid like that restores one's faith in the future."

Peter said, "Right now we are just guessing our way around this. It is possible that we are way off the mark."

"So, what do we do about it?" Benny said.

Betty said, "We should go to the police."

Benny said, "There you go, again. You tell the police your dead husband told you about Vasquez, and they'll surely put you in a rubber room."

"Should we get involved in this?" Eleanor said.

"Marjorie was our friend," Betty said, with insistence. "And Eugene said we had to do something about it."

"Jesus, Eugene," Benny said, rolling his eyes.

"There are some things that happen where one should

not stand by and watch,'' Walter Innes said to Eleanor. ''Though I'm not sure what we can do in this situation.'' He looked to Peter.

Peter shrugged. ''I don't know, either. But I do feel we should do something.''

''Me, too,'' Benny said.

''I think the best place to start,'' Peter said, ''would be with Richard Allan. He spoke freely with us the other day. Maybe he'll open up to us again, if we present to him what we know?''

''Sounds good, Slick,'' Benny said. ''If anybody can get him to talk, you can. We go first thing in the morning?''

Peter nodded. ''It is better to see him at work, than to bring this to his home. And I think we should talk with Jacobson. Find out what his involvement is with Vasquez.''

''What about us?'' Betty said. ''You want us to sit around and wait while you two do all the work?'' The idea clearly was not acceptable.

''I would like to help, too,'' Walter Innes said.

Peter thought about that a moment. ''We are in the in-formation-gathering stage right now. Why don't you get some information on what our friend Vasquez is doing?''

''You mean, follow him around?'' Eleanor asked, ap-parently not taken with the idea.

''Yes,'' Betty said, excitement creeping into her voice. ''Maybe we can find out something we can bring to the police, so they'll listen to us.''

Peter said, ''Betty knows what Vasquez looks like. She could point him out to you.''

Eleanor raised an eyebrow. ''You want me to get into this?''

Peter looked at her a moment. ''Yes.''

Walter Innes said, ''I would gladly accompany you two fine ladies, if you don't mind?''

Eleanor said, "Don't you think all this could be dangerous? As you said, this guy's no Peter Pan."

Everyone went quiet.

Peter said, "The alternative is to sit by and watch as others die. The next death might be one of us. And there's Coral Sands. We still do not know what Vasquez has to do with Jacobson, but Jessie said he was trying to buy the place. That is not good news, given the type of character our Mr. Vasquez is. And the police are not prepared to do anything until they have reason to be pointed in the right direction. We appear to be the only ones that can get them pointed that way." *And off my back,* Peter thought.

"Well," Eleanor said, surrendering with a shrug, "it would be a change of pace around here."

A change of pace from what! Peter thought, incredulously.

The next morning Peter and Benny left in Benny's car. When they drove into the parking lot of Boat Decor, there was only one car there. It looked like Richard Allan's gray Mercedes. They sat in the car a moment before Benny finally spoke. "I guess we better get this over with. I'm getting a little jumpy."

Peter opened his car door. "As you said to me the other day, the worst he can do is throw us out."

"Yeah, well, I'm not too sure that's the worst." Benny took a deep breath, then opened his door and stepped out of the car. Peter followed.

They walked through the door to the building. The secretary's desk was empty. "Looks like Herman's out oiling his muscles," Benny said. He knocked on the office door.

Benny heard Richard Allan say, "Come in." He opened the door and stepped inside, with Peter right behind him. Richard Allan was seated behind his desk. His face went from welcoming to a frown laced with annoyance, then quickly covered with cordiality.

"Good morning," Richard said, and indicated the chairs. "Please sit down."

Peter and Benny each nodded and took a seat.

"You gentlemen look a little glum. Is this visit about Georgie again?"

"You might say that," Peter said, looking for a way to ease into it.

"Well," Richard said, "I had a long talk with Georgie, and he seemed to understand what was going on with Maddie and I. At least, I thought he understood. Maybe I was wrong. Has he come to you with his problems again?" The man was trying to keep it light.

"Where's Mr. America?" Benny said, with a nod in the direction of the door.

"Oh, Herman," Richard said, feeling on the defensive. "He's not here all the time. I believe he will be here this afternoon. Is there something going on with Herman?"

Benny said, "Other than he works for Vasquez, I don't see any problem." Richard Allan's face changed and became guarded, ready for anger.

Damn Benny, Peter thought.

"Why are you two here?" Richard said, suddenly wary.

So much for easing into it, Peter thought. Time for some quick damage control. "It's difficult to be precise. Mr. Vasquez is attempting to purchase the Home, Coral Sands, and we have become aware that you have a business arrangement with him. We were hoping to get some information on the man and his business reliability." Whatever that meant. "You see, we—the residents—are also considering purchasing the Home. Any information you can give us would greatly increase our negotiating ability with Mr. Vasquez."

Richard Allan did not drop his guard. "There seems to be a misunderstanding. I'm not sure where you got your information from, but I do not have any business arrangement with Mr. Vasquez." He paused. "I'm sorry, but I can not help you. I wish you luck in your attempt to purchase Coral Sands."

He wasn't buying any of it, Peter thought. Might as well charge ahead. "I understood that you owe him money."

"Look, what the hell is this all about?" Richard demanded. No mistaking his defenses were up now. "My business is none of your business. I told you I do not have any dealings with Mr. Vasquez. And you'll have to accept that."

"Vasquez is bleeding you dry, isn't he?" Benny jumped in. "That's why you had to kill Marjorie—to get her money to pay him off."

So much for damage control, Peter thought, wryly.

Richard Allan was on his feet, his body stiff with anger. "What kind of crazy talk is that!" He nodded in the direction of the door. "I suggest you two crazy old men get the hell out of here, now."

Peter and Benny rose to their feet. Peter said, "I think it wise if you were to be careful in your dealings with Mr. Vasquez. He is a dangerous man. The police might be able to help you."

"Look," Richard Allan said. "Get the hell out of here, and keep your nose out of my business. It's nosy old men like yourself that'll get somebody killed. Just get out of here, and go about doing what old people do. And leave me and my family alone."

Peter motioned to Benny to leave. As they moved through the doorway, Richard Allan shouted after them. "Don't come around here again! Herman will have strict instructions to hurt you when he throws you out!"

Outside Benny said, "Sorry about that, Slick. Guess I just couldn't hold it in."

"You did defeat the purpose of my being there," Peter said.

"Yeah," Benny said as he got in the car. "It was not smart."

Peter got in the passenger's side of the car and closed the door. "But it was not for naught. We did find out some of what we came for. We just did not get Richard Allan's cooperation."

"Yeah," Benny said, starting the car and backing it out of the parking space. "We know he's got something going with Vasquez, and it's not friendly."

"And he is definitely under pressure, the way he tightened up when you mentioned Vasquez."

"You noticed that, too, huh?" Benny asked, guiding the car out of the parking lot and onto the road. "And what he said about getting somebody killed."

Peter nodded. "But we have nothing we can take to Ardley, yet."

"Maybe we'll get lucky with Jacobson," Benny said.

Jacobson had a small office storefront in downtown Sarasota. He didn't really need a storefront to manage the affairs of the two retirement residences he owned. But the store was located where a lot of potential residents would see, in the window, beautiful pictures of their retirement dreams; and they could stop in and ask questions and get a brochure with those same pictures to take with them. Besides Coral Sands with its prime location near the Gulf, he also owned Camelot Woods in East Sarasota near a golf course. Camelot Woods was made up of individual villas with a central activity hall and dining room, nothing like the elegant hotel atmosphere of Coral Sands.

Pineapple Street had angled parking which permitted more parked cars along the street, but never enough to meet peak demand. When Benny drove down the street, it was early afternoon and there were no parking spaces available in front of Jacobson's office. Not unexpected. What was unexpected was the white Cadillac parked directly in front of the office.

"Looks like Vasquez is here," Peter said. "Which means that the women should be somewhere around." He was scanning the parked cars on either side of the street looking for them. "What sort of car does Eleanor drive?"

"A white Mercedes," Benny said, his eyes searching the street for a place to park. "Looks like we'll have to go around the block to park."

"There they are," Peter said. He spotted the women parked farther down the street. Then he noticed the woman standing in the doorway of the store in front of the Mercedes. It was Alice Chomseky! "That's Alice in the doorway?" Peter asked.

Benny shrugged, his eyes on the road. "Guess they recruited her."

"We will have the whole damn place in on this!"

"You got a problem with that?" Benny said, as he maneuvered the car around the corner. There was parallel parking on this street and there were a couple of open spots near the far corner. "I figure the more the merrier." He pulled the car to the curb.

"I am concerned that someone will get hurt," Peter said. "Vasquez is not a friendly type of individual."

"Don't worry about Alice," Benny said, as he opened the door and stepped into the street. "She can take care of herself. Probably the first thing she learned working in the circus."

Peter opened the door and got out of the car. He was

worried. Somehow this was getting out of hand before it even started. All he wanted out of this was to get something to direct Ardley away from him. Not to put anybody in danger, or get them hurt.

"Look, Slick," Benny said, as he moved in step with Peter who was walking toward the corner. "You're not dealing with kids here. These people are old, but they're not stupid. They know the score. And something like this beats TV."

Peter shook his head and sighed. "Well, let's play it to the end."

When they reached the corner, the white Cadillac was coming down the street toward them. The white Mercedes had its back-up lights on and was waiting for the Cadillac to pass. Alice was no longer in the doorway. The car passed them, and made a right at the corner. The Mercedes backed out, straightened, and drove after the Cadillac. Alice lowered the window and waved to them as the Mercedes went by. Peter shook his head in resignation.

When the two men walked into the storefront there was only one person in the room. He was sitting behind one of the two desks.

"That's Jacobson," Benny said, indicating the overweight man at the desk.

Peter went directly to the desk and put out his hand. "Mr. Jacobson, I am Peter Benington." He saw immediately that there was no recognition in the man's eyes. Wherever Jacobson was, he was not in this room. From the sweat covering his face, and the look in his eyes, wherever he was it was hell.

As Peter watched, Jacobson slowly became aware that he was no longer alone. He looked up at Peter and Benny, frowning to see them clearly, trying to bring the world in focus. "Yes," he said, in a distracted voice, while running his hand through his dark hair. "I'm sorry. Could you come back in a little while? Denise"—he glanced at the other desk—"will be back from lunch and she can help you. I'm having a bit of problem and must leave now." Where he was going, he didn't know. But he had to get out of there.

Peter noticed the man's hands were trembling, and his eyes began roaming about, like an animal looking to escape. The sweat wet his face and stained his shirt. There was a small cut on the man's throat that trickled a rivulet of blood toward his shirt collar. "Are you all right?" Peter asked, with concern.

"Oh, yes. Yes, I'm fine." Jacobson struggled to get some semblance of control over himself. "It's something personal that I must attend to. Please forgive me. Why don't you take a brochure and come back in an hour. Denise, my assistant, should be able to help you then."

Jacobson began to rise from his chair when Peter said, "Vasquez do that to you?" Jacobson stopped halfway up, his hands on the arms of his chair, and peered at Peter.

"Who are you?" Jacobson said, and finished standing. There was fear in his eyes.

"I am Peter Benington," Peter said, "and this is . . ."

"Benny?" Jacobson said. "What is this? What do you guys want?" His voice was shaking, threatening to break. He had had all he could stand.

"What's this about Vasquez buying Coral Sands?" Benny said.

"Yes. Yes," Jacobson said. He rubbed a shaking hand over his face, and collapsed into the chair. "He wants fifty-one percent ownership." Peter could see tears forming in his eyes. "I really don't want to sell. This is my whole life." He looked at them, and for a moment hope glimmered in his eyes. Then his shoulders sagged, and there was only desperation and despair. His eyes slipped away. "I have no choice."

"Maybe we can help you?" Peter said.

Again Jacobson looked at them, again there was a momentary flare of hope. Then the hope was gone, and he shook his head. "I don't think so."

"Possibly we could get the residents together and make you a better offer," Peter said, for something to say at this point.

"You don't understand. This is not open for bids." He sighed a deep, despairing sigh. "He has given me no choice."

"From the look of that cut on your neck he has threatened you," Peter said.

"Look, don't get involved in this. There is nothing you can do." Jacobson was pleading now. "More people will get hurt. I've already told you more than I should have. I . . . I have to work this out myself. Though, God knows how."

"When is he gonna buy the place?" Benny said.

"Day after tomorrow," Jacobson said. "My lawyer will have the papers ready then. Three o'clock he'll be here."

"That gives us two days," Benny said.

"Please stay out of this," Jacobson said. "I'll do everything I can to protect all of you. But you must not interfere. Please."

Walking back to the car, Benny said, "That guy's backed in a corner."

Peter nodded. "And it appears that all of us are there with him."

"You mean that part about protecting us?"

"Yes. With Vasquez in control we may have no Home."

CHAPTER
12

"Just what is all this!" Jessie Cummings said. She was looking at a list Manuel had dropped on her desk. Manuel was standing in the doorway. He always stood in the doorway, as if afraid to enter her office. Or maybe, to be ready to flee. She had wondered about that. A moment before, he had hesitantly stepped into her office, placed the sheet of paper on the desk in front of her, then retreated to the doorway. Once again he had chosen a bad time. She was trying to make arrangements with a caterer to supply the meals until she could find a new cook. And she was in the process of looking up employment agencies to put out the word there was a job open for a cook, when Manuel popped in with this paper.

"It is all that is missing," Manuel said. "You say I should make a list." He shrugged his shoulders, and made an expression indicating it was obvious. "There is the list."

"All this?" She couldn't believe it. How could so much have been taken without anyone seeing what was happening?

"Is complete." He nodded.

"Silver sugar bowl and creamer?"

"Yes."

"Silver salt and pepper shakers?"

"Yes."

"Two silver candlesticks?"

"Yes."

"Incredible," she said. "How could this happen?"

Manuel brought his hands up and shrugged his shoulders. "He is a good thief?"

"Wrong answer, Manuel," she said. "How could somebody steal all of this stuff and no one on the staff see anything?"

Manuel stood there and said nothing.

"Unless," she said, "the staff was in on it."

Manuel shook his head sadly. "No." His look said she didn't understand. "Impossible. The people don't steal. They like working here. It is hard to get a job. But"—he shrugged again, he did a lot of shrugging—"all the time, there are people coming in and out of the kitchen. Anyone could take stuff."

"But, Manuel, this is a *lot* of stuff!"

"It is particular stuff, too," he said.

She looked over the list again. "Yes. This guy's not setting up a restaurant, but it looks like he's setting up a home."

"Yes. I see that, too."

"Any of the staff recently married, or engaged?"

Manuel shrugged. "I don't know."

"Well, whoever it is, he's got good taste."

"Yes. Also, he has initials CS. Maybe."

"The monogram is on the plates and the silverware," she said, thinking aloud. "But not on the glasses."

"Also on the napkins."

"Napkins?"

"Yes. I can not find twelve napkins."

"God," she said, sarcastically. "Did he take a tablecloth, too?"

"No. And no table or chairs," Manuel said seriously.

"Well, at least he's got his own furniture." She sighed. "We have to put a stop to this, somehow. We're looking at a lot of money here."

"Plastic," Manuel said.

"Don't start that again, Manuel."

He shrugged. "Who steals plastic things? Or paper plates?"

"Who needs a dishwasher then?" she said, looking at him.

He shrugged and nodded meekly. "Plastic is not a good idea."

Alice had parked the car down the street from Liebestraum, a small Austrian restaurant which, beside having a full indoor service, had tables under umbrellas outside, off the sidewalk. The white Cadillac was parked outside the restaurant. Vasquez and Herman had gone inside a few minutes before.

"How many is that?" Alice asked.

Eleanor looked at the notebook. She had been writing down the names and addresses of each place Vasquez had gone. "Six. He's got a busy business."

"I wish there was some way to find out what goes on inside when he visits," Walter said.

"Yeah," Alice said, "to be a fly on the wall."

"I'm sure he's not nice to them," Betty said. "Because he's not a nice man."

"Perhaps we should follow him inside," Walter said.

They thought about that.

"Maybe, one person," Betty said.

"We wouldn't be able to wait for them," Alice said.

"Not if we want to keep following Vasquez and his friend."

Walter said, "But it might be a good idea to leave one person inside to overhear what is said. We could come back for them later. Or they could find their own way home."

"We'd need a busload to cover this guy's stopovers," Alice said.

Eleanor said, "Suppose we only do that for a few of them? We'll leave someone inside to try and catch the conversation?"

"Look," Betty said, "here they come now."

They watched as Vasquez came out of the restaurant with Herman and another man. The other man, with his head down, was listening to Vasquez. Vasquez was making gentle hand motions as he spoke—a man making a point, and in no hurry about it. The two men moved away from Herman, to a table beneath an umbrella, the table next to the sidewalk. They were alone, the rest of the outside tables were empty. Except for the one Herman sat at two tables away. Herman had a bottle of beer in his hand and, in his role as bodyguard, was keeping an eye on the two men.

"Too bad we aren't closer," Betty said. "Maybe we could hear what they were saying."

"Yes," Walter said.

They watched for a moment, then Alice grabbed her purse and said, "I got an idea." Before anyone could ask her what it was, Alice was out of the car. She went to the trunk, opened it, and took out the walker. She closed the trunk and crossed the street. On the other side she unfolded the walker, put her purse in the basket, and started moving slowly up the street toward the restaurant. She took small steps and leaned heavily on the walker.

"She is sure a woman of action," Walter said.

Eleanor slid over into the driver's seat. "We should be

ready to pick her up in case something happens." Then, "Damn. She took the car keys with her."

"They are undoubtedly in the purse she has in the basket on the walker," Walter said.

They watched her progress toward the two men talking at the table.

Betty said, "Won't they think it funny, someone walking on the street? I mean, you don't see many people out there in this heat."

"I think the walker would be explanation enough," Walter said.

"I hope they don't recognize her from the Home," Eleanor said.

"What if they did?" Walter said.

As Alice drew close to the outdoor tables she slowed even more, taking tiny steps, so she could be within hearing distance longer. The two men glanced at her as she moved along, then paid no further attention. Just another old woman in a town of old people. She could hear what they were saying.

". . . a partner," Vasquez was saying in his lazy voice. "You don't need to pay me what you owe. See, you sign over to me half the business, equal partners, and the debt is clear. Is that easy."

"I don't know," the other man said, trying to keep the pleading out of his voice. "I can't give away half the business that belongs to all my family. My wife and sons work very hard to make the business. It is not right to do that to them."

"Heinrich, my friend," Vasquez said, his voice getting oily. "Where do you have the choice? You owe me money you can't pay . . ."

"I paid you already four times what I owe you. I can pay no more."

"I explained that to you," Vasquez said, patience his virtue. "You paid me the interest on the money. I am not a bank. I loaned you ten thousand dollars . . ."

"I paid more than the interest. I gave you money toward the ten thousand, but you don't count that."

"I don't accept part payments on the loan. You want to clear the debt, you pay me ten thousand, plus the interest due. Right now that's twelve thousand and getting bigger. You got that kind of money?"

The man shook his head, hopelessly. "No."

"So, we agree you are behind in your interest payments, and you still owe me ten thousand dollars, and you do not have the money." Now Vasquez shook his head. He shook it slowly, with a sad look on his face. "I told you that you had to pay me or I would be forced to have Herman collect it. Herman is a good boy, but he is very strong. You could be badly hurt."

"But my family," he pleaded. "It is their business, too."

Vasquez's face went cold. "Herman could see to it that you do not have a family to worry about. Do you want that?"

The man shook his head again. "No."

Vasquez nodded and said, his voice soft again, "Now, I want your lawyer to draw up the papers giving me fifty-one percent of your restaurant . . ."

"Fifty-one percent! You said equal partners."

"It is almost equal," Vasquez said. "I need to have the extra edge to protect my investment. I don't want you hurting my investment in your restaurant by making bad decisions. You understand that, don't you?"

The man was beaten and looked it. He was slumped in the chair, his head down. "Yes."

"Good," Vasquez said, his voice filled with pseudo-sympathetic understanding. "Day after tomorrow I will come back to sign the papers. Don't try to make trouble now. Herman will be coming with me.''

Alice was so intent on listening she didn't notice the boy on in-line skates coming down the sidewalk until he was right up to her, standing in front of her and blocking her way.

''Hey, lady. Can't walk too good, huh? Why don't you get yourself some skates. Don't need to walk then.'' And he laughed.

A wiseass, Alice thought, *just what I need.* The kid looked twelve or thirteen, in shorts and a T-shirt, wearing a helmet, elbow and knee pads, and a smart expression on his face.

''You want to move out of my way, or you gonna stand there until I faint from the heat?''

''I never saw an old lady fall down before. Might be an interesting experience.'' And he grinned.

By now the men had stopped talking and all three of them were watching Alice and the boy on skates.

Then the kid said, ''You know, you can't do anything. You can't push me out of the way. You can't chase me or anything. I think that's a dumb thing to do, put yourself out here where things could happen to you.''

''What sort of things?'' Alice was getting pissed at this kid.

''Well,'' he said, ''like someone takes your bag.'' He lifted Alice's purse from the basket. ''And takes all your money.'' He grinned again and opened the bag.

Alice took a deep, angry breath, braced herself, and swung the walker into the kid's legs, knocking him off balance. ''Geez!'' the kid cried, as he struggled, arms swinging and legs going, to try to keep himself on his feet. Alice gave the kid a push with the walker and, skates going up in the air, the kid went down on his back on the sidewalk with a yell. Alice stepped forward, placed the walker over the kid—two of the legs on either side of his head, the other two beneath his armpits—and leaned her weight on the walker, pinning him to the ground. "Damn, lady! What the hell you doing?"

The men laughed. "That's the way, lady," Vasquez said. "Kids got no respect today."

"Now, sonny," she said. "You see that crossbar between these front legs. If I lean on this walker a little harder, it will cut into you throat. You understand what I'm saying?"

The kid nodded as energetically as possible under the walker, his eyes wide.

"Good," Alice said, with a smile. "Now, give me my purse."

The boy raised his hand and handed her the purse. She opened the purse and removed a Swiss Army knife. She showed it to him, as she slowly opened the large blade. "I keep this for protection. It is very sharp." The kid just watched, his eyes growing wider at the things Alice left unsaid.

"Ho, ho," Vasquez said, "the lady is armed."

"Way to go, Grandma," Herman said. More laughter from the men.

Alice said, "You got a name, sonny?"

"Ryan. Ryan Knight."

"Now, Ryan Knight, the next time you see me on the street, you cross to the other side. You understand?" The kid nodded, his eyes glued to the knife. " 'Cause if I see you, I'm going to carve my initials in your chest with this knife." She leaned her face down to him. "There are already three other boys with my initials on their chests. Next time you're at the beach, check around, see if they're there: A.C. You look for them." She let her eyes move momentarily toward the men at the restaurant. "See those men over there?" The kid tried to look without moving his head pinned under the crossbar of the walker. "I'm going to let you up now. If you try anything funny, while the ambulance is taking your bloody body to the hospital, those men will be telling the police exactly what happened here. You understanding all of this?" The kid nodded.

Alice stepped back and lifted the walker off the kid. He scurried up onto his feet, and skated out of reach. "Up yours, Grandma!" he yelled, then raced away down the street.

"You are a dangerous lady," Vasquez smiled.

"It's the only way to keep men in line," Alice said, folding the knife blade and putting it back in her purse. Then she straightened the walker and shuffled off toward the street corner.

"I'm glad she's on our side," Walter said in awe. In shock, they had watched the entire scene from the car, not able to speak.

"God," Betty said, in astonishment, "I could never do that."

"I always knew circus people were tough," Eleanor said, admiration in her voice. "But I never knew how tough."

A police car was parked out front when Benny and Peter returned to the Home. *Another death?* they thought at the same time. Benny parked his car next to the police car. They hadn't spoken much on the ride back, each with his own thoughts on what had happened at Jacobson's and what they were going to do next—if anything. "Well, Slick. If this keeps up"—indicating the police car—"Vasquez is going to buy into an empty house."

Peter looked at Benny. "Maybe that is exactly what he wants to do."

Benny raised his eyebrows at the thought. They got out of the car and went inside. A policeman was standing at the front desk talking with Grace. She looked over and nodded at Benny and Peter as they entered.

"Mr. Benington," she said, "this policeman was looking for you."

The cop turned away from Grace and stepped over to Peter. "Mr. Benington, Detective Ardley would like to speak with you. Would you please accompany me, sir?" He motioned with his hand toward the front door and the police car outside.

Peter exchanged glances with Benny, then asked the cop, "Am I being arrested?"

"No, sir. Detective Ardley sent me to get you because he would like to speak with you, sir." Again with his hand, he indicated the front door and the waiting police car.

Peter turned to Benny. "Do you know of a good lawyer? I think I will be in need of one."

"I'll see what I can do," Benny said.

Peter nodded, then walked outside with the policeman following. The patrolman opened the passenger's side car door, Peter got in. The cop then got in the driver's side, started the car, and pulled it out into the street. No words were exchanged throughout the drive to the station.

The police station was unassuming—a simple, brick structure that could have been anything. The police cars parked in front gave away its function. The policeman escorted Peter inside where the air was cool and the utilitarian decor cold. They spared no money on a decorator, Peter thought. Peter was taken upstairs to an office. Ardley was seated behind the desk.

"Good afternoon, Mr. Benington," Ardley said, not getting up. He was sitting with his arms on the desk, his hands together. With a motion of his head, he indicated the chair in front of the desk. "Please sit down." Then to the patrolman, "Thanks. I don't think I'll need you anymore." The cop nodded, and left, closing the door behind him.

"Nervous?" Ardley said.

"When faced with the power of police authority, I see nervous as a normal state." Peter could not get the tension out of his body. His muscles were tight and stressed. He tried to will himself to relax, but it wasn't working.

"You got nothing to worry about, if you didn't do anything," Ardley said.

Peter looked him in the eye. "I have heard too many stories to the contrary."

Ardley smiled. "Overenthusiastic police work, I imagine."

"Are we going to discuss police procedures? Is that what you wished to talk to me about?"

"Where have you been today? I sent the car for you a couple of hours ago."

"I was out with a friend trying to enjoy my retirement," Peter said.

Ardley nodded thoughtfully. "That's a nice place you live in. Requires a lot of money to stay there. Where would you get such money?"

"Frugality and wise investments," Peter said.

"I didn't realize the insurance business paid so well," Ardley said. "I would have steered my son in that direction."

Peter tried to picture Ardley with a family. He couldn't.

"You have any children?" Ardley said.

Peter nodded. "A son."

Ardley kept his thoughtful look. "I received a telephone call yesterday afternoon from a Detective David Benington of the Newark New Jersey police. Your son?"

"Yes," Peter said.

"I have to admit that, at first, I thought it might be you posing as a cop." He shrugged. "It's been tried before. I called the Newark police to confirm he was who he said." He hesitated a moment. "I wondered how a man in your profession raised a son to be a policeman?"

Peter waited. So far the conversation hadn't gotten to the point.

When Peter didn't say anything, Ardley continued, "He asked me for information about a man named Vasquez. Was he getting that information for you, by any chance?"

"Yes," Peter said. *Now we're getting down to it,* he thought.

"Thank you for being honest with me, on that," Ardley said. "I don't suppose you'd tell me why you wanted information on Vasquez?"

Peter thought for a moment, trying to decide how much to tell Ardley about what they had discovered and what they surmised was going on. "I would rather not, right now," Peter said. The police would only get on their case, and tell them to stay out of the way. Leave it up to the professionals, etcetera, etcetera.

Ardley gave him a wise nod. "I didn't think it would be that easy. Let me tell you that this Vasquez is one tough piece of slime. He's into much of the dirty stuff going on in this town. Sarasota is not a big place, but every place has its Tough Tony in one form or another. If you are looking to fence the jewelry through him, I advise you not to. He is a dangerous man. He'll take the jewelry and leave you a floater. I would not like to find you floating facedown in the bay."

"I did not take Marjorie's jewelry," Peter said.

"Yes, yes. Deny everything," Ardley said, sarcasm creeping into his patient tone. "Not very original, I have to say. We always seem to get innocent people in this place.

Sometimes it takes a while before they admit their guilt. But that is rare. We send an awful lot of innocent men to jail.''

Ardley leaned back in the chair, his hands still clasped on the desk. His tone of voice returned to quiet patience. ''We'll see how innocent you are when I get the report back from NCIC. You know, the FBI's National Crime Information Center? So far they have not found any criminal record to go with your name. So, it takes a while for their computers to search for a match on the fingerprints and come up with a name and face to go with them. I'm not holding my breath on that. But I did want you to know you are still our prime suspect in this.''

''Then you've excluded Benny Ashe?''

Ardley snorted a laugh. ''Benny was never a suspect. I didn't bother sending his prints off to NCIC. I told him that to break his balls after he made me get that court order for his fingerprints. The man's been here for fourteen years, *Ms.* Cummings told me, and he's kept his nose clean. Why do I want to dig up some criminal past he might have— small-time, if any? He sure doesn't impress me as a big-time operator. I got enough to handle with the active criminals. I don't need to try and grab a seventy-year-old petty thief. Won't look good on my record, or in the press, me taking in that little old man in handcuffs—for shoplifting thirty years ago—and stuffing him into a prison system already packed to the doors.'' Then Ardley leaned forward and peered at Peter. ''A jewel thief and a murderer is something else again. I'm real interested to see what NCIC comes back with on you. See if there's a record of arsenic and barbiturates in your past.'' He kept looking at Peter, waiting for a reaction he could read.

Peter frowned, but tried to remain nonplussed. ''Barbiturates? I thought you said strychnine?''

"The last one was barbiturates." Ardley looked down at the file opened on his desk. "Mrs. Walden. We got the toxicology report this morning." Then he looked back at Peter. "Changing the poison won't throw us off, you know. It's not original. There hasn't been a crook with an original idea in a hundred years."

"That you know of," Peter said. "Those with the original ideas, you haven't caught." He said it without thinking, and as soon as the words were out, he regretted them.

Ardley gave him a knowing smile. "Like you?"

Peter said nothing.

"Well," Ardley said, "I think your troubles are getting worse, to get back to Vasquez. For a long time we've been trying to clean the streets by putting Tough Tony behind bars. There's one man that deserves to be cared for and fed by the state. Now, if someone could help us do that, we might be forgiving about a little jewel theft. You understand my drift?"

Peter nodded slowly.

"The theft goes on the record as unsolved. And we for . . ." The phone on Ardley's desk rang. He calmly unclasped his hands and picked up the receiver. "Ardley," he said into the phone. He listened for a few moments. "Yeah. Okay." More listening. "I said, yeah, didn't I? I understand. Yeah." And he hung up the receiver. He clasped his hands together again and looked at Peter. "It appears that I should keep my mouth shut sometimes, instead of giving people advice. There's a lawyer downstairs who says you're his client, and he wants to see you right away."

Good old Benny, Peter thought, and wanted to smile, but didn't. No need to aggravate Ardley. The man would only start harassing him more if he did. Besides, he might need the man's good graces soon.

"There isn't anything you'd like to tell me before you leave?" Ardley asked, in his most friendly, sympathetic tone. After a moment, he smiled. "I guess not." Then he sighed. "You can go see your lawyer now."

Peter rose and headed for the door. As Peter opened the door Ardley said, "I'm sure we'll be talking again, Mr. Benington." Peter closed the door behind him and went downstairs. Benny and a harried-looking man in his thirties were standing by the desk near the front door.

"Hey, Slick," Benny said, when he saw Peter. "Got here as quickly as I could."

"Thanks, Benny." Peter smiled. "Your cavalry arrived in time."

The harried-looking man stuck out his hand and said, "Bill Fresno as in California."

Peter took the man's hand and shook it. "Thank you for coming, Mr. Fresno. I appreciate it."

"They all do." Fresno smiled.

"I will not need your services anymore today," Peter said. "If you would send me a bill, I will be happy to pay it."

"Will do," Fresno said. "And here's my card in case you need me."

Peter took the card and put it in his pocket.

"I'll be off. More people to rescue." Fresno smiled, gave a little wave, and left.

"I got my car outside," Benny said. "Figured you'd need a lift."

"Let's get out of here, Benny."

CHAPTER
13

"And you should have seen Alice," Betty said, her eyes wide and alive. "It was so exciting. She was great! She really showed that kid something." They were seated around a table in the coffee alcove bringing Peter and Benny up to date. Peter and Benny had already told them about their visit to Richard Allan and Jacobson. Now, after Betty had told of Alice's adventure, Alice was clearly not enjoying her fame.

"He was just a smartass kid, that's all," she said. "What's the big deal is what I heard them saying before the kid showed up. Seems Vasquez is pulling the same deal on this guy who owns the restaurant. Trying to muscle in on the business, and take it over. A regular entrepreneur."

"Yeah," Charlie said. To Peter's dismay, the group had grown by one while Peter was in Ardley's office. "And he's moving fast. We don't do something, he's going to take over the Home as well. Probably, turn it into a high-class house of prostitution."

"He can't throw us out," Betty said.

Charlie said, "If he can intimidate Jacobson to sell the place, he can intimidate you to leave."

"You mean scare us into leaving?" Betty said.

"Or make it so uncomfortable," Walter said, "you wouldn't want to stay."

"So what are we going to do about it?" Eleanor said.

Walter said to Eleanor, "You are assuming there is something we can do."

Peter said, "Ardley stated clearly that the police have been after Vasquez a long time."

"And they'll be after the guy a long time to come," Benny said. "People are too scared to come out and talk. Afraid they'll wind up dead. That's how something like this works. It's a crime that has to be reported, and testified to, and no one's gonna take the risk."

"But what about all those other people he'll do this to?" Betty said.

Benny said, "No one guy is gonna put his neck and his family on the line to stop Vasquez from hurtin' other people he don't know, and who are probably shmucks anyway."

"That," Peter said, "may not be altogether true."

"C'mon, Slick," Benny said, frowning in disgust, "get real."

Peter said, "If Ardley was able to bring them all together in one room, and introduce them, he might get them all to testify. Safety in numbers, you know." He felt he was on to something. "If one got Ardley the names and addresses of Vasquez's victims, then he would be able to do just that, get them all together. Let them see they are not alone, and let them see all the others who are being intimidated."

Benny said, "You gonna be the one to talk Ardley into doing that?"

Peter gave Benny an assured smile. "You leave that part to me. The first thing to do is find out who his victims are."

"Well," Eleanor said, looking at her notebook, "we followed him around one day and got six addresses, not counting Jacobson and Richard Allan.''

"Good," Peter said. "That's the information we will need to give to Detective Ardley. The more names the better.''

Walter cleared his throat. "How long do you think we should keep this up?''

"Yeah," Benny said. "We don't have much time.''

Charlie said, "Any agreements made under duress can be nullified.'' When they all looked at him, he shrugged, "A salesman has to know these things.''

"I thought you were in charge of an office in Europe for some company or other?'' Benny said.

Charlie nodded. "ConFab, in Munich. It was a sales office, primarily. I ran it. But I didn't get there without being in the sales ranks for many years. Worked my way up.''

"Well," Benny said, "by the time they get the agreements thrown out, Vasquez could turn this place into a dump.''

"We have two days before the contracts are signed,'' Peter said. "Let's see what we can find out. Maybe we'll have enough to take to Ardley.''

Charlie said, "You say this guy works out of a restaurant downtown?''

"Yeah, Pancho's," Benny said.

"It has very good food," Betty said.

Charlie said, "Well, let me tell you. I was a good salesman in my day. And I know bartenders know what's going on. I'll go down there tomorrow and see what I can get out of him.''

Walter said, "If this Vasquez thinks we're checking him out, it could be trouble.''

Charlie smiled broadly. "I said I was a good salesman. That's all I'll be—a salesman on vacation. A little talk, a little drink, a little friendly chatter, and all that.''

"Yeah," Benny said. "Just remember, this guy kills people, and we're people."

Peter said, "All right, then. Let's do this again tomorrow. And we will meet here to compare notes."

Eleanor said, "We'll go over to his house early in the morning and spend the day with him."

"And Alice"—Peter smiled—"no more showing off."

Alice made a face.

Benny said he would meet Peter and Eleanor in the lobby and they would all drive to Caroline's for dinner. Peter and Eleanor showed up before Benny, and sat on a sofa to wait. Eleanor was wearing a tan skirt and a blouse with a patternless array of muted browns, reds, and greens. There was a gold necklace at her throat, and her hair was done in a casual look. Peter marveled at the myriad ways a woman's hair could be styled, each giving a different quality to the woman. "This is my dining-out blouse," she smiled. "Any food I spill on it won't show." Peter had on his Florida outfit—a soft blue shirt, white slacks, and shoes.

Eleanor confided to Peter that this was the first time, in the three years she had been there, that she had seen Benny serious about a woman. She thought it was cute, a man his age getting palpitations over a woman.

"An old man," Peter said, "is a young man trapped in an old body." He gave her a playful smile. She returned the smile, and he hoped it held the promise he thought he saw there.

When Benny met them in the lobby they almost didn't recognize him. He had on a new pair of gray slacks, gray hush puppies, and a light red silk shirt—and no baseball cap.

Benny was fidgeting with his shirt, not sure if he'd done

the right thing, getting new clothes. "What do you think?"

"You look absolutely wonderful." Eleanor smiled with approval.

"A gentleman about town," Peter nodded.

"But you forgot your baseball cap." Eleanor grinned. "I hardly recognized you with hair."

Benny held up his hands to them. "Look guys. You got to make me look good in front of Caroline. So, no cracks, no put-downs, okay?"

With a smile to each other, they both agreed.

Outside Benny led them to his car, clean and bright.

"You even got the car washed and polished," Eleanor said. "She must be a very important lady. You're definitely giving her the wrong impression of you."

Benny looked embarrassed. "C'mon. You said no cracks."

"We aren't at her house yet." Eleanor smiled. "I'll have to get it all out of my system before we get there."

Benny made a face. "Great."

They got in the car, and Benny drove it out of the parking lot and onto the road.

"Where did you meet this wonderful woman?" Eleanor said.

"Why do you have to know?" Benny said.

"Well, I want to know where I can go to meet a charming man," Eleanor said.

"At the supermarket," Benny said, reluctantly.

"Any particular aisle I should stand in?" She was clearly enjoying this teasing.

"She was sitting on the bench with her groceries waiting for a bus." He threw it out, not wanting to discuss this at all.

"And you offered to drive her home," Eleanor said. "How gallant of you." She turned to Peter. "If I were waiting for a bus would you offer to drive me home?''

"Any gentleman of breeding would," Peter said with a straight face.

Benny was suddenly very uncomfortable about having these two to dinner. "There's something I got to tell you. She lives in a mobile home."

Eleanor shrugged. "Is that a problem?"

"Well"—he hesitated—"it's not a fancy one, if you know what I mean?"

"Don't worry," Eleanor said, "there is no shame in where a person lives."

"And"—this was the hard part—"please don't say anything . . . well . . . just please don't?"

"A mystery?" Eleanor said. She had never seen Benny so worried.

"We can talk after we leave, okay?" Benny said.

"It is a deal, Benny," Peter said, pretty sure of what Benny was trying to say.

Benny drove into an old mobile home park, Oak Manor. The homes were all single-wide and close together. Here and there in the park was a glowing new double-wide home that looked like a mansion next to the sorrier old single-wides. He pulled the car into the carport of a pale-yellow single-wide with brown trim around the windows and the door.

Nervous, Benny looked at them. "This is it. Now please don't say anything . . . er . . ."

"I'm sure everything will be just fine," Eleanor said. "You said her name is Caroline?"

"Yeah, Caroline Sandersen. A very nice lady," Benny said.

"You think we can go in now, Benny?" Peter said. "Or is this a drive-through dinner?"

Benny gave him a pleading look.

Peter raised his hands. "That's the last crack I'll make until we leave."

Benny took a deep, fortifying breath and opened the car door. They got out of the car, and followed Benny up the aluminum steps to the front door. Benny rung the bell. There was a long moment before the doorknob turned and the door opened. Standing before them was a little, frail lady in a blue print dress. Her gray hair was short and neatly styled. Amid the frail wrinkled face were blue eyes that danced with life.

"Oh, do come in," she said, her voice as frail as her body. "Please do come in." She stepped back, pulling the door open wide.

Benny pulled open the screen door, and stepped inside with Eleanor and Peter behind him.

"Oh my Lord, Benny, you look absolutely marvelous!" Caroline said, looking Benny up and down. Benny fidgeted uncomfortably. Then she turned to Peter and Eleanor. "And these must be the wonderful friends you told me so much about." Caroline smiled.

Benny introduced them. Peter was taken with her blue eyes sparkling with excitement.

"It is sure a pleasure to meet you both," Caroline smiled. "Please come in. Dinner is ready for the table. So please have a seat at the table. I just need some strong man to open the wine bottle. With my arthritis, I find it difficult to manage that." The soft Southern drawl in her voice was like gentle, soothing music.

"I'll help you with the wine," Benny said, and gave Peter and Eleanor a worried glance.

Separating the long living room from the dining area was a hip-high divider. Beyond the dining area was the kitchen, a counter separating the two rooms. The place was clean and cheerful. No luxuries here. Peter noticed it was decorated with early Salvation Army furniture similar to Benny's apartment.

They followed Caroline to the dining area, and Benny continued on with her to the kitchen where the wine bottle stood on the counter.

The table was laid out exquisitely with fine china, beautiful glassware, silver flatware and candlesticks, on a lace tablecloth. Surprised, Peter and Eleanor both stared at the layout on the table.

"Don't you think it just marvelous?" Caroline said, as she carried a plate of vegetables to the table. "A sweet, romantic man gave it to me." And she smiled at Benny, who avoided their eyes.

"It is beautiful," Eleanor said. *And very familiar,* she thought. So this is where the things are going. No wonder he was worried about what they might say.

"He even had the plates and silverware made with my initials. He's such a charming thoughtful man." Caroline gave Benny a loving look. Benny blushed and busied himself with the wine bottle.

"He has exquisite taste," Peter smiled. "I see the napkins are monogrammed, as well."

"Yes. He simply thought of everything," Caroline said, and went back into the kitchen.

Peter and Eleanor sat next to each other and exchanged secretive smiles. Caroline came back in with a tray of carved beef, surrounded by small potatoes, and placed it in the center of the table. Benny brought in the wine and poured everyone a glass, while Caroline finished bringing out the bread and salad. Benny dimmed the lights and lit the candles. Then Benny and Caroline sat down. She just glowed with pride at the way the table looked.

"It looks so elegant," Caroline said, beaming with the joy of it. "Benny said that everyone needs a little luxury in their sorry lives. I thought this was much too extravagant, but now seeing it laid out on the table, it is just as perfect as can be." She looked with admiration at Benny and touched his face gently with her hand. "And he was so very right." Benny beamed at the affection. She returned her hand to the table, and turned to them. "It makes dining so civilized." They all agreed.

They ate and chatted like old friends who had come together after a long time and were trying to catch up on each other's lives. Peter and Eleanor found that Caroline had married a gentlemen farmer who turned out to be more a gentleman than a farmer. He inherited the farm and the money from his father, and it took him thirty years to lose it all. Penniless, five years later he died of disappointment and a stroke. Caroline's salvation was the life insurance money. She'd found work in an office which kept her from starvation, and now she survived on her retirement check and Social Security. And she had vowed never to depend on a man again. She looked soft eyes at Benny. "Present company absolutely excepted." Benny blushed again.

Peter learned that Eleanor was actually born and raised in Florida. "A regular Florida Cracker. There are only a few of us around, but our ranks are growing. Most people you meet in Florida are from someplace else." And she had been married the first time when she was seventeen. Her parents did not care for the boy she married, and threw her out of the house. When the marriage did not work out (she didn't elaborate), she made her own way in the world, doing anything from waitressing to managing a boutique, before she met Matthew: a kind, sweet, older man who took her away from all that.

Dinner finished, Caroline said, "Now, you two gentlemen go out on the lanai, while us ladies clean up here. Then we'll have you in for dessert. Pecan pie all right?"

Peter smiled. "Pecan pie is the only true dessert."

"Oh," Caroline said, smiling and waving her hand at him. "You are such a smooth talker, Peter. Good breeding, no doubt."

Benny poured a brandy for himself and one for Peter, and they went on the lanai, a screened porch that overlooked a dark lake. The sun had set while they were dining so leisurely. Now, the lighted windows of the other mobile homes reflected warm yellow off the water. Benny grunted. "Anything that collects water in Florida is called a lake. In Brooklyn this would be a large puddle that would slow traffic a little." This one was about a hundred yards long and thirty wide.

"But it is nice here." Peter sighed and sipped at his brandy. They had stretched out on the lounge chairs.

"Thanks," Benny said. "For not saying anything in there."

"You mean about the dishes?"

"Yeah."

They sat quietly for awhile staring out at the lake, then Peter said, "Time for a confession."

Benny let out a deep sigh. "Yeah. Guess so." Neither of them looking at the other, they kept their eyes on the dark lake. "Well, I hope you understand what I'm going to tell you, because it took me a while to understand it myself. You see, Caroline is a real lady, you know what I mean?"

"Yes, she has poise and charm," Peter said.

"And she's struggling here, and not complaining. You gotta admire that. She gets her Social Security and forty bucks a month from her pension. I'd be bitching all the time. But she takes it with a smile, and thinks she's lucky. She's some woman."

Peter sipped his brandy and said nothing. It was clear

that Benny was infatuated with the lady, and there was nothing he could say to that.

"I guess I wanted to do something for her. Something to help her. I offered to give her some money and she turned me down. Not angry or anything. She's got a way of saying things that makes them sound like they're surrounded with flowers."

"It's the charm of the Southern lady," Peter said.

"To go out and buy her the dishes didn't seem right. The gift had to have more value to me. It had to be earned with risks. Things that come too easy don't have real value. You know what I mean? I know this sounds stupid, but like a knight going out to win a fight with some shmuck, instead of paying the guy off and telling him to go home. The whole thing had to be something I could have said to myself that I won it like in battle. Like I was worthy of her attention." Benny snorted. "Listen to me. I sound like some nut."

"Sounds very romantic to me," Peter said, smiling in the dark.

They were silent for awhile, then Benny said, "I'm gonna talk to Jessie tomorrow and pay for the stuff. I just had to get it that way, earn it."

Peter nodded in the dark. "I understand, Benny." And he sipped at the brandy. It was nicely warming his spirits.

More silence, then Peter said, "While you're in a confessing mood, Detective Ardley, he told me he didn't send your fingerprints to Washington. So, how about you telling me how much of that story you gave me was true." He could hear Benny chuckle.

"Didn't believe me, huh?"

"I'm sure some of the truth was buried in there somewhere," Peter said. He swirled the brandy in the glass and sniffed the woody aroma.

Benny chuckled again. "You are pretty slick, Slick. Well, I *was* in the Witness Protection, I think they called it Witness Security Program. I was in Virginia, when that shmuck with the gun showed up and tried to kill me. It didn't take a rocket scientist to figure out that I wasn't going to be safe even in the hands of the Marshals. There's always somebody who can't resist the temptation of money for information. So, I got my act together and when the time was right, bugged out. That was when I came down here. Nobody knows where I am. I was afraid that my fin-gerprints would ring a bell in Washington, and the Marshals would come looking for me, along with Bobby Dee's guns. Some people don't forget, and I think Bobby Dee is one of them. That's if he's still alive." Benny sipped his drink, and lapsed into silence.

"Interesting," Peter said. "But that brings up another question. Where did you get all the money to stay down here?"

"Slick, were you ever a cop? You got an eye for the details, if you know what I mean."

"Bobby Dee's money, you said."

"Yeah, that's right. After Angela's death"—he paused and sighed—"Bobby Dee came to me, and told me he was sorry things got out of hand. He was out to teach me a lesson, but not to have the jerk kill Angela. Wasn't good business to let someone rip you off without getting back at them. He said he'd taken care of the guy, if that made any difference. I acted like a broken man. But I was planning my own revenge. I contacted the District Attorney and told him what I had to offer; Bobby Dee's head on a platter, in return for being put in the protection program. It was a couple of days before he contacted me and told me it was a deal. We made arrangements for me to come to them on a certain day. I packed up my stuff, mostly memory stuff of Angela and me. Then the night before I was to meet them, I hit Bobby Dee's place, and walked with almost two hundred big ones of his money. You see, the problem with gangsters is money. They got to keep it in cash because anything else the government watches and the Feds'd be on them in a whistle. So, the next day I disappeared into the protection program with one suitcase of memories, and one of money.'' Benny shrugged in the dark. ''Simple as that.''

''And you kept it in cash,'' Peter said. Benny was something else, he thought. Well, he sighed, tough guys grow old, just like jewel thieves.

''Yeah. The Marshals didn't know what they were carrying around for me. So, when the time came to jump out of the program, I took the suitcase of money with me. So, in a way, Bobby Dee's paying for my retirement.''

''Again, I must say, that you are taking a risk telling all this to me,'' Peter said.

''Nah, I don't think so,'' Benny said, and sipped at his brandy. ''Now, suppose you tell me how you became a jewel thief?''

CHAPTER
14

Peter didn't know whether it was the brandy mellowing his good judgement or that he just wanted to tell someone. Maybe it was the sudden rapport he felt with Benny. Maybe it was just old age and the need to talk about one's life to someone. He didn't know and didn't much care.

"Elliot Osborne," Peter said. "The man who showed me the way."

Benny took a gulp of brandy, feeling its pleasant warmth trace its way down inside then reach out to his limbs, and waited. One thing he knew, you had to be patient, and let a guy tell his own story his own way.

"I was working in an insurance company, National Security, for about two years. I was twenty-two, and making what I thought was good money for my age, ten thousand five hundred dollars a year. One day, I received this telephone call. It was lunch time and I was the only one in the office. The man on the other end said that he wanted to return a necklace that he'd stolen. He said he wanted twenty thousand dollars for it. And he'd call back later with instructions on how the exchange of the necklace for the money would be done. I thought the man was a crackpot. When Potter, the supervisor of the office returned from lunch I went in his office and told him about this nut that had called.'' Peter chuckled as he recalled the scene.

''I was surprised as hell when he said I should take the instructions down, and he would arrange for the cash. I said, 'The man's a thief and we're going to pay him!' I couldn't believe it. I remember what Potter said to me because it changed my whole life. 'Son,' he said, 'you have to remember one thing. We are in the business of making money. That necklace was insured for one hundred thousand dollars. We turn that man in to the police, and we're out one hundred thousand dollars we have to pay to the insured. We pay him and we're only out twenty thousand. That much we'll make up easy by raising the premiums on all the insurance policies for jewelry and valuables. Nobody will notice. And the people who pay are those rich enough to have insurance on valuables. They won't miss it one bit.' ''

''Sounds to me,'' Benny said, ''like the guy was encouraging people to steal.''

''He had an answer for that one, too,'' Peter said. ''We turn the man in and no one else will come to us with their stolen valuables. The crooks will still steal, but they will fence the stuff for ten cents on the dollar, and we'll be out thousands. If they know we'll pay, they'll come to us, and we'll save money and no one gets hurt.''

''So, who was Elliot Osborne?'' Benny said.

''The man called back and gave me instructions for the delivery of the money. He said a messenger would meet me with a package in return for the cash.'' Peter laughed softly. ''Potter told me to handle the exchange. Said it was good experience. Elliot Osborne was the messenger. He came complete with a messenger's uniform and all. I gave him the envelope with the money, and he gave me the package with the necklace. Once that had been done, I invited him to lunch. He smiled and accepted. He said later that he thought I had a pair of balls to invite him to lunch. Elliot Osborne was the thief posing as a messenger. After the long talk we had with lunch he 'took me under his wing,' I believe that's the expression. I mean, here's a man who made twenty thousand dollars in a few hours, and I would barely make that in two years. I knew I was at the wrong end of this deal. So, Elliot Osborne and I came to an arrangement. I gave him a list, names and address along with the items that were insured, and he'd commit the thefts and come to me for the exchange. I got a piece of the payoff each time." Peter chuckled.

"No one ever caught on. Not even my wife. And my reputation for getting back stolen valuables was made. Ten years later I became a consultant to the insurance industry. Every company was happy to give me their lists."

"And you never stole anything yourself?" Benny said, incredulously. "That's what you want me to believe?"

"Elliot taught me a lot," Peter said, smiling to himself. "At times I would cut him out and do the whole deal myself. I cultivated an English accent and . . ."

"You mean Sherlock Holmes was right!" Benny grinned and shook his head in wonder. "Unbelievable."

"Yes," Peter smiled, "he was right." And strange, Peter thought. But in the past few days he'd come upon some pretty strange things all around. He swirled the brandy in the glass and sniffed at the aroma. "With the accent I could pass myself off as a minor duke or something, and it helped me to move in some wealthy circles on my own time. Occasionally, I'd let my own fingers do the walking. I even had some luck in Europe." Peter swallowed the last of the brandy in his glass. Damn, he felt good. "I've never told anyone about this before. And I don't know why I'm telling you.''

Benny said, ''Because I'm the first person you can trust not to repeat it.''

''Yes,'' Peter said, ''maybe that's it. It just feels good to share it. No, that's not the word. I'm not sure what the correct word is. But, it's nice not to have to put up a front anymore.''

''You never got caught?''

''Oh, I had a couple of close calls. But I never had identification in my own name. Not that that would have helped if I'd gone to jail. But people, especially wealthy people, are reluctant to press charges once they have their valuables back. They frown on publicly stating what fools they were to let themselves be victims, and publicly telling everyone who they were and how rich they were. They prefer to keep all that among themselves. So, they avoid going to court.''

''Who's going to court?'' Eleanor said. She had just opened the door to the lanai.

''Vasquez, we hope,'' Benny said.

''Let's leave Mr. Vasquez out of this evening,'' Eleanor said. ''Caroline sent me to tell you gentlemen that coffee and dessert is now being served.'' Then she lowered her voice. ''Benny, she is a wonderful woman. I truly like her.''

''Yeah, she is,'' Benny said. ''But like the old saying goes, if she takes up with the likes of me, then you got to question her judgment.''

''Come on.'' Peter smiled, pulling himself up out of the lounge chair. ''I'm ready for some pecan pie.''

The rest of the evening was pleasant, and on the way back to the Home, Benny explained to Eleanor about the dishes and that he was going to contact Jessie in the morning and pay for them. She liked the romantic notion of

taking risks for "his lady love." Back at the home, Benny
went off to his apartment, leaving Eleanor with Peter.

"I had a nice evening," she said to him. They were
sitting in lounge chairs out by the pool having a cigarette.
The pool lights gave the whole scene a soft glow.

"I couldn't have chosen a more charming lady to spend
it with," Peter said. He liked the way the light illuminated
her face, giving a jewelled sparkle to her eyes. He liked the
company of women. He found them interesting. They saw
the world so differently from men, with none of the male
posturing. They were more open and honest about their
emotions. A friend had once said that they were wonderful
aliens. Because only an alien would get all sparkly over a
bunch of flowers. With Peter there were times when a special woman came along who touched him uniquely and
powerfully. Eleanor was one of those women.

She smiled at him. "I happen to like you very much,"
she said in a soft voice. A voice that had a "but" in it.

He sat there quietly, conscious of the "but," yet not
wanting to say something that would blow his chances with
this woman. He truly enjoyed being with her and, for the
time being, that might have to be enough. "I am strongly
attracted to you, Eleanor. I think time may only strengthen
that feeling."

She smiled again. "I hope so." Then she stubbed out
the cigarette, and rose from the lounge chair. "Time for
me to get to bed. Tomorrow is a busy day. I'll see you in
the morning, Peter."

"Good night, Eleanor," he said, giving it all the sweet
emotion he felt.

It was while they were at breakfast the next morning that
Herman showed up. Grace came to them in the dining
room. Benny, wearing his New York baseball cap, had just

asked Betty if she had contacted Eugene last night.

"Yes," she said, exasperated. "I asked him how this was all going to turn out. He said, 'Win by a nose.' Honestly, that man sometimes is such a bother."

"There's a man to see you both," Grace said, to Peter and Benny. "He says he's Richard Allan's assistant."

What the hell? Peter thought. He and Benny exchanged questioning looks.

Peter said to Grace, "Is he driving a white Cadillac?"

"Yes," she said. "It's parked right outside the front door."

There was a moment of thought, then Peter said, "Please tell him we'll be right with him."

Grace nodded and went away.

"What was that all about?" Eleanor said. She had seen the disturbed look on their faces.

"I don't know," Peter said. "And I don't like this." He looked to Benny. "You think Richard Allan sent him to see us?"

Benny shook his head. "I don't think so. Sounds like Vasquez wants to talk to us."

Peter frowned. "How did he get on to us?"

Benny shrugged. "I don't know, but if Herman was here to hurt us, he wouldn't have driven up to the front door."

Eleanor looked at the others. "I guess we'd better get out to the car and follow them."

Peter was concerned that things were getting out of control. But he didn't know what to do about it. He said, "We will give you a couple of minutes to get to the car before we leave."

Betty, Eleanor, Walter, and Alice got up from the table and left the dining room.

"Now, Benny," Peter said, "I would like you to hold

your temper. At least until we find out what this is all about.''

Benny nodded. ''Don't worry about me, Slick.''

But Peter did worry. Benny was unpredictable and arrogant. So far nothing serious had come of his acting up, but there was always a first time.

They waited a few more minutes, then got up from the table and walked out to the lobby. Herman, in a loud short-sleeved shirt, his arms folded, his size and bulk dwarfing the residents who passed by him, stood calmly at the front desk waiting for them.

''How are you doing, Muscles?'' Benny said, and Peter groaned inwardly. ''You wanted to see us?''

''I was sent here to bring you to visit a gentleman who wishes to talk with you.'' Herman was quiet when he spoke. There was no emotion in his delivery. An automaton delivering a message. He let his size and strength give power to his words. He unfolded his arms, and extended a hand toward the front door. ''The car is outside.''

''A good place for it,'' Benny said with a chuckle, and went through the front door with a worried Peter following. Herman came out last, moved deliberately to the Cadillac and opened the back door. Benny and Peter climbed in and Herman shut the door. He got in the driver's seat, started the car, and drove it out of the parking lot into the street.

''Must be tough, holding down two jobs, eh, Herman?'' Benny said.

Herman kept his eyes forward and said nothing.

''Which one do you like best?'' Benny asked. ''Sitting on the boss's lap taking dictation or holding Vasquez's hand while he gets in the car?''

No response from Herman. Peter, however, was rolling his eyes. He wanted to tell Benny to keep his mouth shut, but knew it would not do any good.

"Or do you do other things for Vasquez, like wipe his ass and kiss his boo-boos?"

Herman's expression didn't change, but he looked at Benny in the rearview mirror.

Peter leaned over to Benny and whispered in his ear, "What the hell are you trying to do?"

Benny, annoyed, waved Peter away. "Big man like you kissing ass is got to be bad for your ego. What do your friends say about it behind your back?"

Herman reached over and pressed a button on the dashboard, a dark window rose out of the back of the front seat and closed them off from him. Benny smiled and shrugged. "Guy's not interested in conversation is he?"

Peter sighed, relieved that the taunting had stopped. "Maybe he isn't paid to talk."

"Maybe he never learned enough words." Benny grinned and shrugged.

They drove about twenty minutes before Herman pulled the car into a driveway that cut through a pink stucco wall, and maneuvered the car to the front of a two-story house, white stucco with a rust-red barrel tile roof. They could see the Gulf of Mexico beyond the house. Herman got out of the car, opened the back door, and signalled them to get out.

"Man's got a great vocabulary with his hands," Benny said, and climbed out of the car. Peter got out on the other side. Herman indicated they should follow the walk around to the back of the house. Benny led the way, Peter right behind him, with Herman bringing up the rear. The grounds were landscaped in lush, healthy plants, and there were huge live oaks that shaded the house. In the back there was a broad patio covered with an awning striped in green and white. Vasquez, wearing a white terrycloth jacket over white bathing trunks, was seated at a table on the patio, a tall drink in his hands. Vasquez saw them come around the side of the house with Herman. Herman indicated they should step up on the patio, and he remained standing where he was.

"Good morning, gentlemen," Vasquez said, giving them a cheerful smile, his voice easy and soft. "Please have a seat." He indicated two empty chairs at the table with him. There was a tall drink on the table by each chair. They sat down and looked at the drinks.

"Piña coladas," Vasquez said. "I know it is early in the day, but, for this climate, it is such a refreshing drink at any time. Please drink, they are not poisoned."

Benny wasn't too sure. Peter sipped the drink and let the icy liquid cut the dryness in his throat.

"We have not personally met," he said. "I am Eustaquio Vasquez." He pronounced it "hay-ooh-stack-ee-o." "To my friends I am known simply as Tony. And you are?"

"Benny," Benny said.

"Peter Benington."

"I know your names, but I was not sure who of you they belonged to."

"May I ask for what reason we are here? I don't remember ever coming in contact with you before," Peter said.

"Me neither," Benny said.

"Well, I am aware that you both know Herman." He turned his head momentarily in Herman's direction.

"Richard Allan's secretary," Benny said. "Hope his shorthand is better than his looks."

Vasquez gave Benny a condescending smile.

"And he's not much of a conversationalist," Benny added.

"He is paid not to talk," Vasquez said, and smiled at his own remark. "I am also aware that you appear to know me, do you not?"

Peter and Benny sat quietly, Peter sipping the piña colada, Benny with his hands folded in his lap.

"Yes." Vasquez shrugged. "Well, Mr. Allan has brought it to my attention that you are trying to meddle in my business."

Peter almost choked on his drink, anticipating a smart reply from Benny. But Benny remained still.

"You are old men," Vasquez said. "You should be doing what old men do. There is not much life left for you. Enjoy it, as the other old people do. Take in the sun, play golf—however you wish to spend your time. Let the world be run by the young men. Those of us strong enough to make the decisions and operate the systems that serve everyone." Vasquez stopped speaking and waited for some reaction from the two men.

Again Peter looked with trepidation at Benny, and again Benny kept his mouth shut, much to Peter's relief.

"You do understand what I am saying, do you not?" Vasquez said. When they didn't reply, he said, "Perhaps I should make things a little clearer. Old people should stay out of the way because they are weak and fragile." He shrugged. "They break bones by just falling down. It is sad to see such things happen when they have such little time left to live." He turned to look at Herman. "Herman, over there"—he turned back at them, his voice still like oily velvet—"is one of the persons who protect my business. They are well-meaning, but"—he shrugged—"overzealous. And they do not know their own strength. Sometimes people get hurt by accident. It is sad. But one must admire the dedication of these men. Is difficult to get such dedication from employees these days."

"What kind of business are you in?" Benny asked. Vasquez was too much of a wiseass for Benny to sit quietly any longer.

Vasquez smiled slowly. "I think we have spoken enough. Thank you both for coming to visit with me. Herman will take you back to Coral Sands."

"You gonna keep the name after you take Coral Sands over?" Benny asked, his face in a hard frown. Let him know we're on top of what's going on. See how he digests that.

Vasquez's smile disappeared. "Herman, take these two gentlemen home." The change in Vasquez's look was enough to stir cold fear in Peter.

"I guess the audience with the Pope is over," Benny said with his smart mouth. Vasquez gave Benny a look that was a promise that he would remember Benny, then Vasquez ignored them.

"Come," Herman said.

"I told you," Benny said to Peter, indicating Herman. "He don't know enough words."

Benny and Peter rose pushing their chairs back, the feet of the chairs making a rubbing noise over the rough patio floor. Herman stepped off the path and indicated they should go past him to the front of the house and to the car. Once around the side of the house, Peter said, "My mother used to call your problem a 'trouble mouth.' You open it and it brings trouble."

Benny chuckled. "My mom just said I had a smart mouth."

They got in the car with Herman and drove silently back to the Home. They were afraid to speak for fear Herman could hear them even with the glass partition up. Herman drove up to the Home and let them out at the front door. Without a word, Herman drove away. It was then that Peter saw Alice's car on the street take off after the white Cadillac. Peter waved frantically trying to get their attention without success.

"Damn," Peter said, under his breath.

"What's up?" Benny asked.

"I was trying to flag down the women, to stop them from following the Cadillac," Peter said.

"Why?"

Peter sighed. "We are in over our heads here, Benny. And Vasquez has all the weapons."

"C'mon, Slick," Benny said. "He's just a wiseass."

"Benny, it is not as if we were a SWAT team or commandos. Vasquez was correct in calling us a bunch of old people"—he didn't like to admit to being old—"who have stepped into a dangerous jungle. And some of us are likely to be hurt. I think we should stop what we're doing until we can reevaluate this situation."

"You mean, back down because Vasquez is scary," Benny said.

"Before, Vasquez did not know we existed. Now he will be looking for us. And I'm afraid he will notice the car following him. He could hurt them if he did."

Benny sighed, his resistance giving way. "Yeah. I suppose you're right."

Peter said, "We could try giving Ardley what we have. It might be enough."

"Wishful thinking, Slick."

"It's all we have."

"We'd better stop Charlie," Benny said. "He's liable to talk himself into center stage. Charlie is a bit of a blowhard, and he likes the drink. He's liable to swallow enough to loosen his tongue. And now that Vasquez knows about us, the man's gonna have his people sniffing the air for somebody nosing around."

"What time does the restaurant open up?"

"Eleven," Benny said.

Peter checked his watch. "It's just a little past ten. He couldn't have gone yet."

They went inside and searched for Charlie. The search lasted close to a half hour, but the man wasn't around. Grace had not seen him leave, but that didn't mean anything. She didn't take note of everyone's comings and goings. They looked everywhere inside and out, not once but twice. Charlie was not around.

Finally Peter said, "We'll have to head him off at the restaurant. Stop him before he can talk his way into trouble."

Benny said, "Let's do it."

They went outside and climbed into Benny's car, now glowing with its clean shine. Benny revved the engine and moved the car out at an uncomfortable speed, Peter groping for a handhold. "Benny, it'll do Charlie no good if we are taken to the hospital and miss him at the restaurant."

CHAPTER
15

When they got to the restaurant Benny found a parking space two doors down. The white Cadillac was not around, but there was a parking space in front of the restaurant with two red cones holding it. Peter pointed to Benny's hat. Benny removed the cap and tossed it in the back seat. His hair was indented with a ring where the cap had sat on his head, and there was a tuft of hair sticking up in the back. They left the car and went into Pancho's. Inside was a dark-haired young man wearing a white shirt and a decorated red vest that Peter assumed was to make him look Mexican. The man asked if they wanted a table. There was no one at the bar and only two people at one of the tables. The back half of the restaurant at the far end of the bar was closed off with one of those moving walls. Where the hell was Charlie?

"Not much of a crowd?" Benny said.

The young man said, "It is early. But we do not do much of a lunch crowd, except in the season when the snowbirds fill up all the restaurants."

Benny looked at Peter for what to do next.

"We will have a table," Peter said.

The man nodded, took two menus off the small desk next to the door, said, "Follow me, please," and walked into the dining room.

Benny said, in a low voice to Peter, "Let's get over there by the window. Looks like we can see who comes in from there."

Peter indicated to the maître d' the table Benny had suggested. The young man shrugged and said, "Certainly," placing the menus on that table. They seated themselves so that Benny could see the bar and the entrance; Peter had a view through the front window. "Can I get you something to drink?" the young man said.

"Coffee regular," Benny said.

"And I will have decaffeinated, please," Peter said.

The man nodded and walked away.

"I hope Charlie wasn't planning to come here for dinner," Benny said.

"We will wait here for a few hours, if necessary," Peter said. "If he does not show, we will have to think of something else."

The young man in the vest brought them their coffee. "Take your time." He indicated the menus lying on the table. "When you're ready to order a waiter will be here— soon, I hope. He's running a little late today."

They nodded their understanding, and the man left.

"By the way," Benny said, "I straightened everything out with Jessie this morning. She said I nearly gave Manuel a heart attack the way things were turning up missing. She was sure Manuel would want to know how I did it. I asked her to keep it all under her hat. Manuel'll have to figure it out for himself." He grinned. "No use giving away trade secrets."

Peter kept looking out the window, scanning the street for any sign of Charlie. He was halfway through the cup of coffee when the white Cadillac pulled up to the parking space with the red cones. Herman got out of the car, moved the cones, got back in the car, and pulled it all the way into the space. Peter turned his head away as Vasquez got out of the car. He didn't want to be seen. "Vasquez is here," Peter said.

Benny looked over at the entrance. When Vasquez came in, and the young man with the red vest greeted him with, "Good afternoon, Mr. Vasquez," Benny scrunched down, and put his hand to his forehead, covering his face. He left two fingers apart so he could see. Vasquez, all in white— white shirt, slacks, and shoes—nodded unsmilingly at the young man, and walked past him. He didn't look like a happy camper, Benny thought. Herman, doing his slow, muscled walk, strutted in behind Vasquez. The bartender, a big, well-built man with sandy hair, stopped cleaning a glass and gave Vasquez a small smile and a nod. Vasquez and Herman walked down toward the end of the bar and out of Benny's sight. He heard them open the wall that closed off that half of the restaurant, then heard it close.

"Are you gentlemen ready to order?"

Benny took his hand down and looked up. A guy with a white shirt, black vest trimmed in gold, and black trousers, stood over them smiling.

Peter said, "Another decaffeinated for now, please. We have not looked at the menu."

Benny said, "Me, too."

When the waiter left, Benny said, "We keep drinking coffee, and I'll have to move closer to the bathroom."

Peter gave him a small smile, and looked out the window searching for Eleanor's car. Sitting down as he was, it was hard to see beyond the few cars near the window. "Maybe we should alert the girls?"

"Charlie's the guy we have to catch first," Benny said.

"We can catch up with them when we get out of here."

"Unless Vasquez leaves before Charlie arrives?"

Peter was looking at Benny and saw his eyes grow wide as he looked over Peter's shoulder. Then he made a weak smile and gave a nod. Peter was apprehensive about turning around to see what Benny was looking at.

"You'll never guess who just came in and went back toward Vasquez's den," Benny said.

Peter waited, then said, "Who?"

The waiter appeared and placed two fresh coffees on the table. "We're waiting for someone," Benny said to the waiter. "We'll call you when we're ready." The waiter nodded a smile and left.

"Chris," Benny said. "The waiter at the Home."

"Chris!"

"He just came in, saw me, and waved, then went in the back."

"Chris and Vasquez." Peter frowned at Benny. "That man has people everywhere." The thoughts were tumbling all over themselves, struggling to come together. "Eugene said that Vasquez was responsible for the killing in the Home . . ."

"Do you believe that guy, Eugene?" Benny said. "Doesn't stay dead 'cause his wife needs the help. I still don't really believe that stuff."

Peter nodded. "I have come across stranger things. I did not want to believe them, either. But I could not deny them."

"Yeah," Benny said. "And Eugene certainly has been eerie coming up with that name like that."

"Yes," Peter said, "Very convincing. And if he's right and Vasquez is our man, then you just saw the man who could have delivered the poison."

"Geez," Benny said, looking once again over Peter's

shoulder. "He seemed like a nice guy." He hesitated. "Hey, he recognized me here. You think he'll say anything to Vasquez?"

Peter shook his head. "I don't know what the man knows about us. He may not even think to mention it, unless Vasquez tells him about our visit this morning."

"Oh," Benny said. "Here come the girls and Walter!"

Peter turned around. Betty, wide-eyed, turned from looking at the empty bar to look over the tables and saw the men. She looked at Eleanor and pointed to them. Then she came over doing her best to hold down her excitement. Eleanor, Alice, and Walter, leaning on his cane, followed her. When Betty got near to them she said, in an excited whisper, "Did you see who came in here just now?" She sat in one of the empty chairs. Eleanor took the other, and Alice brought over two more chairs for herself and Walter.

"Yeah," Benny said.

"We were coming in to look for a telephone to call you," Betty said. "We didn't know what to do."

Eleanor said, "Especially after your visit to the man this morning. What went on there?"

"Basically," Peter said, "he wants us to stay out of his business or we're going to get hurt."

Eyes raised. Then Alice's face turned into a hard frown. "The twerp. Just who the hell does he think he is?"

"Easy, now," Peter said. "We are the over-the-hill gang. And we are involved in something that is way out of our league. The man is dangerous, and he has dangerous people working for him. We should take a hard look at our position before we do anything rash."

Eleanor said, "You think we have enough to go to Ardley with? I mean, besides the names we have, the man also threatened you?"

"Give me a break, Eleanor," Benny said. "Who's going

to take the word of two paranoid old people against that guy? And what'll he get, a slap on the wrist for scaring the poor old people?''

Peter said, "I am not sure if the six names are enough. But it is all we have. I think we should remove ourselves from this situation right now, and go see Detective Ardley.''

Walter, leaning on the head of his cane with two hands, said, "I feel it is most prudent. We don't know what the police already may be doing. This information may be enough to at least get them to do more.''

Alice said, "But, what about the Home? How are we going to stop him from taking over the Home and throwing us all out on the street?''

"Yes," Betty said, "Eugene said we would win by a nose. He doesn't lie to me.''

Benny said, sarcastically, "But he don't make himself clear, either. Does that mean we should stop and go to the police, or keep doing what we're doing?''

Eleanor said, "How can we do that now that we know Chris is connected to Vasquez? I think that's information for the police.''

"Yeah, there's Chris," Benny said. "A snake in the weeds. Peter thinks he was the guy slipping poison to everybody.''

"Gee," Betty said, "he could have given it to one of us. We could be dead, too.''

"Then," Benny said, in a sarcastic tone, "maybe you could ask Eugene what the hell he meant.''

"Well," Walter said, "that accusation may be a bit rash. We don't know why Chris is here. He could be involved with Vasquez in a lot of ways. Perhaps he is paying him money that he owes, like everyone else?''

They fell silent, each trying to deal with the questions,

and with the realization that Chris, that nice young waiter, was somehow connected with Vasquez, the man who was going to ruin their home, and who Eugene said was responsible for the poisonings.

"Well," Alice said, "we can't just sit here all day. I don't think it's smart that we're here if that twerp has threatened to hurt us."

"Yes," Peter said. "We came here to intercept Charlie before he talked himself into trouble. Why don't you all go home? Benny and I will wait here a little longer until we catch Charlie. Then we'll deal with Ardley."

Alice said, "If you're going to the police, I think we should all go with you. The police don't listen to one old person. There's gotta be some numbers before we get their attention."

Walter nodded sagely, then stopped in mid-nod, his eyes looking up.

"Please," a voice said, and they all looked up. Herman was standing above them like a giant. He was now wearing a tan suit jacket with no lapels, the front hanging open. "Mr. Vasquez would like you to join him for lunch." For emphasis, Herman held the jacket open, and they understood why he was wearing the jacket, to hide a very large gun tucked in his belt.

They all looked nervously to each other, hoping someone would make a decision. Though there were six of them, Peter was sure Herman could hurt every one of them without much sweat, old bones breaking all over the place. And the whole incident would be dismissed as crazy behavior by a bunch of old people at a restaurant. Peter sighed—"I think we should accept the gentleman's invitation to lunch"—pushed his chair back, and stood up. The others hesitantly did the same.

Herman herded them past the bar to the movable wall at

the far end. The bartender gave them a curious look as they went by. The wall was open partway in the center. Herman indicated they should go inside. Benny led the way, the others following single file through the opening. Vasquez was seated at a table, a plate of colorful food in front of him, a large white napkin tucked into the throat of his shirt.

Vasquez raised an eyebrow at them, "Herman, did you bring in the whole restaurant?"

"They were all at the same table with these two," Herman said, indicating Benny and Peter.

Vasquez gave him a small shrug. Then to the group, "Please sit down," he said, in his sleepy voice. He turned to Chris standing off to one side. "Pull up another table and some chairs for my guests."

Herman pulled the walls closed while Chris dragged over a table and butted it against the one Vasquez was seated at. Then Chris and Herman brought over four more chairs and arranged them around the table grouping. Benny took the chair immediately to the left of Vasquez, then Eleanor, Alice, Walter at the end opposite Vasquez, then Betty with Peter at Vasquez's right. Herman took up a position next to Walter between the table and the way out through the movable walls. Chris stood between Eleanor and Alice, a little behind them.

Vasquez looked over the group of expectant faces. Then to Peter and Benny, "I didn't expect to see you two so soon after our visit this morning." No one responded. "You are my guests. Would anyone like something to eat? Chris can serve you. He is a very good waiter, I am told." Vasquez was almost smiling at Betty's horrified look at Chris. Again no one responded. He shrugged. "No one is hungry? That is too bad. The food here I recommend. It is very good, and much safer than at Coral Sands." This time he did manage a small grin that lasted a moment. "I hope you do not mind if I eat in front of you. I don't like the food to get cold." Using a fork, he cut a piece of what looked like an enchilada, scooped it on the fork, and eased it into his mouth. They sat there watching him savor the taste, chewing quietly, then swallow. He picked up the glass of red wine and took a large gulp.

"Now"—he sighed—"my business is with Mr. Ashe and Mr. Benington. So, I do not see any reason for the rest of you to stay."

Before anyone could make a move, Alice said, "Up yours, twerp. We're all in this together."

God—Peter groaned—*a Benny in drag.*

Vasquez was visibly stunned, but his expression quickly shifted to recognition. "Ah, yes, the tough lady with the walker." He looked at Chris standing next to Alice. "Be careful, she is armed and dangerous." He laughed. Herman and Chris laughed, too.

Vasquez put on his sleepy-eyed look, and surveyed the group. "Very well," he said. Then he looked to Peter. "So, you have recruited a little gang of your own. That is too bad. I hoped we could keep all this between the two of you." He looked at Herman and Chris, then looked back at the group, and shrugged. "This does not pose a great difficulty, though."

"Why did you kill Marjorie and the others!" Betty blurted out, her voice shaking, her face angry and red. "Nice people like that! Why!"

Peter was surprised. He hadn't thought she had it in her. *Well, that should seal our fates.* Peter groaned inwardly. If they had had a chance of getting out of this before, Betty certainly took care of that. He saw in the eyes of the others that they, too, understood this. Suddenly his heart began to beat erratically, and he worried that it might choose that moment to fail him.

Again Vasquez looked stunned. He sighed audibly, and his expression went cold. "I do not know these people you speak of."

"Yes, you do," Betty insisted, hanging on. "You poisoned them." Vasquez looked at Chris, then looked back at Betty. "Eugene told me you did it."

Vasquez looked around the group and his eyes rested on Walter. "You are Eugene?"

Benny said, "Eugene's her dead husband. He talks to her."

That wiped the cold look from Vasquez's face. He frowned a moment in thought. "Her dead husband talks to her?"

"Yes," Betty said, hard, "and he knows all about you."

Vasquez's face relaxed, and he looked around at the group. He had reached a decision. He gave Betty one of his almost smiles. "Perhaps I can arrange for you to join him, this Eugene."

"Eugene said you killed them for the money!" Betty's emotions were cranking way up.

Vasquez shrugged carelessly. "It is a good reason for killing."

Might as well jump into the fray, Peter thought, there didn't seem to be anything to lose now. "Did Richard Allan pay you to kill Marjorie, his mother-in-law?"

"Why would he do such a thing?" Vasquez said. "He is not such a person."

"As the lady said, for the money," Peter said. "His wife inherits all her mother's money."

Vasquez looked around the table at each of them, studying them, sizing them up. Then he looked at Peter. "I do not work for Mr. Allan. I work for me."

Benny leaned forward resting his elbows on the table. "How much was he into you for?"

Vasquez shrugged. ''Her money would be enough to pay me what he owes.''

''So, killing her was your idea!'' Peter said, getting into it. ''That way you knew you would get your money.''

Vasquez shrugged, he had made his decision. ''The man was falling too far behind in payments.''

Walter said, ''What of the other three women you had killed? Were their families indebted to you?''

Vasquez looked at Chris. Chris said, ''I told you, I didn't do the last one.''

''Jacobson didn't owe you any money,'' Benny said, reaching for understanding.

To Peter things suddenly began to fall into place. ''You were putting the muscle on Jacobson by trying to affect his business! You thought a few people getting killed would chase away some of the residents and put a scare into Jacobson and pressure him to sign over half of his business before matters became worse.''

Vasquez looked at Peter calmly but didn't say anything.

''It did not work, though, did it?'' Peter said. He was excited that things were coming together so rapidly, and he was struggling to make sense out of them. ''Or did you change your mind?'' He hung there a moment and more pieces fell into place. ''Yes, of course! The police. You did not anticipate the police getting involved. Old people die all the time and nobody suspects anything. But Marjorie's daughter trying to prove negligence by the Home exposed the murder. So you decided to threaten Jacobson directly!''

Vasquez gave a little shrug. ''Women, they are unpredictable.''

Frowning, his gaze hard on Vasquez, Benny said, ''What were you going to do with Coral Sands? It don't sound like the kind of business that would interest you.''

Vasquez gave Benny the beginnings of a smile. He was

enjoying these old people, their playing cops, they don't know they're dead. "Businessmen need a nice place to stay that has *all* the advantages."

"Gambling and prostitution," Benny said, to the others at the table, "is what he's talking about."

Betty exploded, saying, "You were going to take away our home!"

Vasquez shook his head slowly. "It is not 'were', it is 'will,' madam."

Betty stood, her anger getting out of control, her face fire red. "No you won't, because Eugene said we will stop you!"

Vasquez chuckled. "Your dead husband . . ." Then Benny hit him.

Christ, Peter thought, *he hit him!* Peter couldn't believe what he'd just seen.

Benny's left hand had come off the table and punched Vasquez in the face hard enough that the man and his chair fell backward to the floor. Everything froze for an instant, everyone was shocked, stunned by this. Then things happened. Eleanor sent an elbow back into Chris's groin. With a grunt of sudden pain he doubled over. Alice grabbed his hair and, using her body weight, slammed Chris's face into the edge of the table. Peter was rising from his chair to get in the fray. Betty was frozen, her eyes wide with disbelief, her anger gone. It took Herman a moment to act. By then Walter was holding his cane at the center with both hands. He brought the cane up, the handle catching Herman under the chin causing him to falter, then Walter drove the tip of the cane into Herman's stomach. Herman let out a grunt of pain and reflexively doubled over grabbing at his stomach. Walter stood and brought the full weight of the handle of the cane down on the back of Herman's head, and the man collapsed like a bag of rags to the floor. Peter reached Herman's body and took the gun from Herman's belt.

"Very interesting bedside manner, Doctor," Peter said, his heart dancing around. At this point he was sure everyone's heart was racing.

Walter, flushed with excitement, looking down at Herman's body on the floor, said, "You wouldn't know how many patients I've had that I would have enjoyed doing that to."

Peter walked around the table to where Vasquez lay on the floor. The man was moaning and holding his face, blood running through the fingers.

Walter came up next to Peter. "I will take that," he said, reaching for the gun in Peter's hand. "You'd better call the police."

"There's a phone by the bar where you come in," Eleanor said, grunting and out of breath as she and Alice dragged Chris across the floor to lay him by Vasquez. There was blood running from Chris's nose.

Peter gave Walter the gun. "How bad is he?" Peter said, indicating Vasquez. There was a lot of blood.

"Well," Walter said, studiously looking down at the man, "in my professional opinion, I'd say Benny broke his nose. There's a lot of blood, but not much damage. It appears likely that Betty's husband was referring to this nose." Walter then looked at Benny. "How is your hand?"

Benny looked appraisingly at his hand, flexing the fingers. "Seems okay."

Walter said, "I suggest you have it X-rayed just to be certain. Old bones are more brittle." Then to Peter, "Now, I do think you should call the police. I'll keep Mr. Vasquez—how do they say it?—'covered' while you're gone." The tremor in Walter's hand worse than usual, he pointed the gun at Vasquez still lying on the floor.

"Hey, old man," Vasquez said, in a muffled voice

through his hands, his eyes wide on Walter's trembling hand holding the gun. "Be careful. That gun could go off."

"I'm not the least worried," Walter said, "because, you see, it isn't pointing at me."

"If you shoot him," Benny said, "we got six witnesses'll say it was self-defense."

Peter walked back toward the wall. Betty was standing stock-still, her hands on her cheeks, her eyes wide and looking around. Peter stepped over Herman and pulled the walls apart enough to step through.

The bartender was at the far end of the bar. He was leaning his hands on the bar talking to Charlie, who had a mug of beer in his hand. They both looked over as Peter entered. The bartender's face snapped quickly from a question to determination. Charlie, seeing this, slammed the heavy mug on the bartender's hand, mashing the man's fingers on the bar.

"Geez!" the bartender yelled, grabbing his injured hand. Charlie, on his feet, rapped the man on the side of the head with the mug, sending the bartender staggering back against the wall of liquor bottles, bottles and glasses crashing around him as he slumped to the floor.

The maître d' turned at the commotion. As Peter went behind the bar toward the bartender, Peter pointed and shouted at the maître d': "Stay out of this!" The man stayed where he was, and he stopped the waiter who ran in from the dining room. "Charlie, call the police," Peter said, indicating the phone on the wall. The bartender was sitting on the floor, dazed, nursing his smashed fingers. Peter picked up a whiskey bottle by the neck, and stood over the man as Charlie punched 9-1-1 into the phone.

Two nights later, Jacobson threw a dinner party for them at Coral Sands and invited everyone. It was a classy, catered affair out by the swimming pool, complete with a string trio playing soft music, and a champagne fountain that Elaine Singleton spent a lot of time at. Benny brought Caroline who was agog at Coral Sands. "You darling man, you never told me how wonderfully charming this place was," she said to him. "It must be like living in a grand hotel." Benny beamed.

Jacobson made a toast to the "Gang of Seven", as he called them, who had saved him from ruin. And the Gang of Seven spent most of the evening telling their story over and over as people came up to them.

Fred Astaire showed up and was dancing the night away with any woman game enough to try.

Tweedledee and Tweedledum were there, eating and drinking along with the rest. "I didn't know they could stand," Benny grinned. "I never saw them outside the gazebo."

Peter overheard the two old men talking about how they don't make old people like they used to. "When I was a kid, old people knew their place," Gray Hair said.

"Yeah, the cemetery," Sailor Hat said.

"No, sitting on the porch in a rocker, or sitting by the window looking out."

"Like the family pet," Sailor Hat said.

Finally, as the evening wore on, Peter was able to get Eleanor away from the crowd to the gazebo. Peter brought glasses of champagne for Eleanor and him and moved two of the chairs close together.

"Exciting evening," she said.

"I don't know if I can stand all this hero stuff." He grinned.

"You seem to be holding up very well."

"I hear that it wears off after a while, until no one recognizes you in the supermarket anymore." Then Peter said,

"Did you know that I have been here a week and have yet to see the beach?"

"That's too bad," Eleanor said. "It is very peaceful at the beach."

He smiled. "I could stand a little peaceful after this past week."

"Perhaps you and I could do a little celebrating of our own? We'll pack a lunch and take some chairs to the beach."

"When?" Peter said, anxious, but not trying to show it too much.

"Well," she said, "tomorrow sounds like as good a time as any."

Then in a soft voice filled with meaning, Peter said, "Are we getting closer?" He slipped his hand in hers. She didn't resist. Instead she held it firmly.

"I feel I'm getting very close to you." Her eyes, sparkling with the lights of the party behind them, looked deeply into his.

It was at that moment that Grace found them. "Peter," she said, "Detective Ardley is here to see you."

Now? Peter thought. Peter looked at Eleanor and he groaned. What was it his father used to say? When things were going well, it means you don't know what's going on. Peter said to Eleanor, "I want you to hold that look and that thought until I get back. Now, don't go away on me."

She smiled warmly. "I'll be right here waiting."

Peter followed Grace to the lobby where Ardley was standing by the front desk.

"I'm sorry to interrupt your celebration, Mr. Benington, but I must talk with you, if you don't mind?"

What the hell was he supposed to say to that? Peter thought. He shrugged.

"Outside, please?" Ardley said, indicating the front entrance.

"Sure," Peter said, and followed Ardley through the front door.

Outside Ardley stood close to Peter and spoke in low tones. "First, I want to tell you that, once they all heard about you and your friends testifying against Tough Tony, every one of his victims started talking their heads off. Tough Tony will be off the streets for good. I thought you'd like to know that."

"You're welcome," Peter said.

Ardley grunted and gave a small smile. "Chris Lassiter, whose real name is Tony Pico, says he had nothing to do with Elizabeth Walden's death. He doesn't mind admitting to killing the other three people, but says he isn't going to take the rap for somebody else. *Ms.* Cummings"—stressing the "Ms."—"told me about the Waldens, and Elizabeth Walden's Alzheimer's. Personally I think Tony Pico killed her, and that's the way it will be handled. As far as I'm concerned that case is closed."

Peter suddenly felt there really was a human inside Ardley. "Thanks," he said.

Ardley shrugged.

"What about the waiter, Carlos?" Peter said. "Wasn't he the one who recommended Chris, this Pico person, to take his place at the Home?"

"People can be persuaded to do a lot of things," Ardley said. "We're looking for Carlos Ortega in the bay. We suspect that once he served his purpose in getting Pico the job at Coral Sands, Tough Tony got rid of him. Tied up loose ends." Then he said, "Speaking of loose ends, you don't have to worry about Mrs. Boyd's jewelry. Richard Allan confessed that he approached Mrs. Boyd a few months back for money for his business. Actually, to meet some of the payments Tough Tony was demanding on the loan. She took him to the safe-deposit box, and gave him some of her jewelry, which explains why we found his fingerprints in the box. Mrs. Boyd told him not to tell her daughter about it. There was enough animosity between them already, and that would have only aggravated it.''

''I had told you that I did not do it,'' Peter said, with a smirk.

''Well,'' Ardley said, ''I just thought I'd let you know what was going on.''

''Is that it, Detective?'' Peter said, thinking of Eleanor waiting for him in the gazebo.

''Yes,'' Ardley said. ''Enjoy your evening.''

''Good night, Detective,'' Peter said, and turned to go.

''There is one more thing,'' Ardley said. ''Do you know a man who calls himself Harvey Benton?''

Peter felt his blood go cold. He turned back to Ardley. ''No,'' he said, through the lump that tightened his throat.

''Watson Bigelow?''

Peter shook his head, but couldn't trust himself to say ''no'' with any confidence.

''Eustace Conway?''

Again Peter shook his head.

Ardley shrugged. ''Thought you might have come across him in your business. You see, I got this fax from NCIC today.'' He took a folded piece of paper from his back pocket, unfolded it, and held it out to Peter. Peter took it, and looked at the picture of himself, a mug shot from twelve years ago. ''They said your fingerprints matched this guy. He was arrested for jewel theft a few times. Used all those names. You recognize him?''

Peter had all he could do to shake his head. Ardley was toying with him. He knew that, and he knew his life was over. Eleanor was going to wait alone in the gazebo for a long time.

"Seems there's a warrant outstanding on him. He missed a court appearance on some jewelry theft. The charges were dropped. But they're still looking for him for skipping bail and contempt of court."

"No," Peter said, his voice weak. "I do not recognize him."

"Funny how they come up with a fingerprint match, isn't it?" Ardley said. He took the fax sheet from Peter and looked at it. "You know, in a way, this guy looks a little like you, too." He let that comment hang in the air where both of them could look at it. Then Ardley looked Peter in the eye. "You know, you can't trust these computers. They're always making these kinds of mistakes. Could really ruin a guy's life." He slowly tore up the fax sheet. "Sorry to trouble you, Mr. Benington. I'll let you go back to your party now." He nodded. "You have a good evening." Then Ardley headed to his car in the parking lot.

"Good night, Detective," Peter said. He wanted to kiss the guy.

"You're welcome," Ardley said, got in his car, and drove away.

When Peter went back to the pool area he found that someone had put soap in the champagne fountain, and it was a mountain of bubbling suds.

For the first time since he arrived, Peter laughed aloud.